FORTY TWO
SHORT STORIES

RICHARD WEALE

For my friend Angua
Happy 42nd Birthday
"Life, the Universe, and Everything"

FORTY TWO

Published in United Kingdom 2024

by FGO Publications, Gloucestershire, England

Copyright © 2024 by RICHARD WEALE

> Stories by their very nature are
> creations of imagination and fantasy

THESE ARE NOT CHILDREN'S STORIES

This book is produced subject to the condition that it shall not, by way of trade or otherwise, be lent, resold, hired out or otherwise circulated in any form without the publisher's prior consent in any form of binding or cover other than that in which it is published and without a similar condition including this condition being imposed on the subsequent purchaser.

All rights reserved. No part of this publication may be reproduced, stored in a retrieval system, or transmitted in any form or by any means, electronic, mechanical, photocopying, recording or otherwise, without the prior permission of the publisher.

ISBN 9798303358782

CONTENTS

The Apothecary	1
Eloise and the Silver Dragon	3
Checkerboard	13
The Bubble	17
Bad Crap City	19
Spice	21
Old Friends	25
Film Noir	27
Here's Johnny	29
The Brush	31
The Adventures Of Benji Mouse	32
The Leaves	44
Vigilante	46
The Old Man	54
The Laughing Man	56
Eloise and the Grumbly Ghost	57
Forty Two	71
Billy Whizz	73
Jane	75
Aunt Gertrude	77
The Taste Of Heaven	79
Philistines	82
Eloise and the Water Serpent	84
Also by Richard Weale	113
Acknowledgments	117

THE APOTHECARY

THE OLD APOTHECARY coughed a reluctant ball of phlegm into a grimy handkerchief. 'Goddamn spiders,' he thought. There is a modern myth that everyone swallows on average, nine spiders a year during their sleep. If you had whispered this fearsome statistic to the apothecary he would have laughed. The crackling wheezing laugh of a man with webs on his larynx.

"Nine," he said gratingly to Moth, his apprentice. "Where did you hear such rubbish? Nine hundred more likely," and that was that.

Moth scampered back to his dirty straw mattress and whimpered pathetically, his mouth clamped shut, wheezing through his snotty nose.

"And that won't help," the old man added sadistically as if he knew Moth had his lips sealed tight, "they'll crawl through your nostrils and ears too."

Moth was slightly relieved at the Master's bile. He knew the second part of this to be a lie. He was often sent down into the well to train his weakling spirit, tightly holding his breath in the freezing dark water, and knew from the pressure the water exerted on his ear drums, that there was no way in there for water or spiders. Still he subconsciously squeezed his nostrils tighter just in case. It didn't help that his Master, the Apothecary was famous throughout the land for his many remedies made from the distillations of spider venom.

'Twenty four srumples of bat faeces dissolved in three fluid ounces of Howler venom.' Moth read the instructions by candle light from the old grimoire, the moulding parchment pages giving off a sour smell of dust and decay. Three fluid ounces sounded a lot even for a relatively giant spider like the Howler, named not for its call, for everyone knew that spiders were silent creatures, but the sound they made when the mallet hit them to extract their venom. Moth, like you and I, had thought that subtler methods would be used, like drawing it out from the spider's fangs with a brass syringe and needle, but this was the Middle Ages where subtlety was rare and venom extraction done by wooden hammers. It was true that the actual venom was little, but what it lacked in quantity it made up for in toxicity, and it was mixed with fish oil both for economy and preservation. So three fluid ounces it was. Moth put the two ingredients together in to the ceramic mortar and ground the mixture to a fine paste with his lovely black granite pestle.

    How Moth loved his pestle. When not grinding potions he kept it lovingly in the breast pocket of his leather jerkin where it pressed comfortingly against his chest. Only one more place was better. The perfect fit it made clasped in his closed fist with the bulbous polished grinding end protruding from his clenched hand. Difficult to see, especially in a dark alley, but devastatingly effective when driven against an unsuspecting temple or Adam's apple, for despite his fear of swallowing spiders, as well as an apprentice Apothecary, young Moth was indeed an apprentice Assassin.

ELOISE AND THE SILVER DRAGON

ONCE UPON A TIME there was a Princess called Eloise. Her best friend was a beautiful white stallion called Rupert.

Rupert was a magnificent wild horse that had been captured by Jagerd The Black, her father the King's, most trusted advisor. He had been on a special quest in the service of the King when he had become lost in an enchanted forest full of Dragons and other magical monsters. Jagerd had been attacked by goblins, and lost his horse. He had been wandering, cold, hungry, and alone, when he came into a clearing in the forest, and there he was, this magnificent horse, head bowed as it drank at the lake.

Disturbed by the strange man's approach, the horse lifted its noble head and held the warrior's gaze. Something strong and magical passed between them and Jagerd was never the same after that day.

Suddenly with a mighty roar, out of the forest leapt a great monster, a Crawzgon, with the snarling head of a wolf, the hard-scaled body of a serpent and the wings of an eagle, and attacked the horse. The horse, for as yet Rupert hadn't been given a name, reared on his hind legs, struck at the creature with his hooves to defend himself, and whinnied loudly. Without a moment's hesitation, Jagerd, trusted Captain of the King, leapt forward, drawing his sword as one, and with a single cut of his mighty blade, cut the roaring and slavering head of the Crawzgon from its huge and powerful shoulders.

Eloise looked up at the great head, stuffed and mounted, on the wall of her castle bedroom and shivered with a frisson of excitement as she imagined the sword of Jagerd slaying the monster and saving her beloved Rupert.

Every morning, whilst the rest of the castle slept, Eloise dressed in her winter riding gear, and slipped out quietly through the sleeping castle, down a secret stairway, tiptoeing through the lovely warmth of the kitchen and out through the snow to the stables where Rupert would be waiting.

Feldon the assistant groom would be there, having saddled the horse. He was usually to be found holding his halter in one hand whilst his other held a biscuit in his palm for the horse to gently nibble. Not that Eloise was pampered, well not for a Princess anyway, because most of her morning, after her ride, was spent helping Feldon muck out all the stables, cleaning the tack and brushing down and caring for the horses.

Afternoons were lessons. Sword and archery, with the Weapons Master, Nogan, magic with Zagoop the King's wizard, strategy with Jagerd, and a whole host of different teachers and mentors who were slotted into her busy young life.

But now, this time with Rupert, was her favourite. Racing through the woods, snow falling from the branches with the speed of their passing, the rising sun lighting up the falling flakes like a million glittering diamonds. Young Feldon, who also doubled as her bodyguard, rode hard behind her on his beautiful chestnut mare, Andromeda.

Together the Princess and her protector raced through the early morning woods, Rupert taking the wooded terrain in his stride, leaping over fallen trees and frozen streams. How she loved these early morning rides. Holding the reins firmly in her strong young hands she let out a yell of pure joy, and digging her heels into Rupert's steaming flanks, the feisty young Princess encouraged her horse even faster, to a gallop, folding herself down on to his neck, so Rupert's mane tickled her cheek as she avoided getting swept off by the lower hanging branches.

The King was in his counting house, counting out his money. In reality, ruling the land was a difficult thing and caused the King, Eloise's father, a great deal of hard work and sleepless nights. A great King needs to manage the land, making sure he can feed his people today, whilst setting aside enough food to see through the possibly difficult tomorrows. He must consider and provide for the defence of the realm, the upkeep of the castles, his guards, and soldiers. Maintaining the King's roads, the functioning of the towns and villages, the wellbeing of their citizens, all these were the concern of a good and caring king, as Eloise's father surely was.

In the King's southern lands, a great and terrible dragon called Zoltan had been terrorising his people from his fastness in the mountains. Dragons had a reputation for loving and hoarding treasures, especially precious gold and jewels, but the King's major problem was the dragon taking livestock to eat, and sometimes even children. It was bad enough for the farmers to lose pigs and sheep, but last week the Miller's little girl, whilst playing a reckless game on the Mill water wheel, had been taken.

Clambering up on the slowly moving wooden structure, she had deftly reached the top, jumping from paddle to paddle on the moving wheel. Careful not to slip on the wet wood, she balanced with ease as she stretched up in triumph waving to her younger brother watching below.

Just at her moment of victory a great shadow came down out of the azure, and the horrified little boy watched, as a great silver beast flashed down out of the sky and with amazing precision snatched the triumphant girl from her lofty perch and flew upwards and away. The little boy had a final glimpse of kicking legs in the dragon's maw and then his sister was gone.

Eloise was very anxious about her Father. He was looking grey with worry. Six more children had been taken. Zoltan had clearly developed a taste for them. The King had sent a company of his finest soldiers to attack the mountain stronghold of the great silver dragon. However, the company commander, an experienced old warrior called Roderick, survivor of many campaigns, seemed to have underestimated his opponent, who had burst out of his stinking lair, and burnt them all to a crisp with one long roar of fire.

The King, as well as losing a formidable fighting force, now had many widows and orphans to care for, the often unseen side of the heroics and bluster of a soldier's life.

Eloise watched her Father at the end of the dinner table, joylessly toying with his food, and decided it was time to play her part in the life of the royal household, and step up her own contributions to the effort.

Eloise tiptoed down the rocky corridor. There was no light, but she had spent all night mastering a few of Master Zagoop's easier spells, and the night vision spell was one of her favourites. Still, she was discovering that sneaking around the castle at night was a lot easier and safer than finding her way into the dragon's lair.

The smell, a mixture of ashes, sulphur and burnt meat, was overpowering.

Now that she was so close, she realised she didn't even have a plan. A few spells, a very sharp doubled edged dagger, a lot of determination, and guile were her resources. Jagerd had always taught her to be spontaneous in the moment, but if she ever got back to the castle she vowed she would pay a lot more attention to his lessons on strategy.

She had managed to give Feldon the slip. He would never have allowed such foolishness, and she realised with a pang of regret that she may have caused his death warrant. She suddenly had a belated flash of understanding on Jagerd's lesson of the chain of events. How did he put it? "It is about understanding the ripples that are created, when you throw a pebble into a still pond." That was it.

Rupert, she had left tethered near the foot of the mountain, with a little hay, and by a stream for water.

A sudden wash of heat and light brought Eloise back to the moment. Muttering silently the spell of invisibility, she palmed the handle of her blade for courage, and stepped through into the void.

The Dragon, Zoltan, admired the girl. He had been aware of her from the moment of her decision at her father's dining table. He had been entertained by her preparations. Impressed that one so young could master three spells. Having lived for thousands of years, one was so very rarely truly entertained. Leaving the precious little horse so close was careless. He looked forward to a snack later, but tonight he was dining on little girl, and a Princess at that.

Stepping into the vast cavern, Eloise took little comfort from her spell of invisibility. She felt exposed, as if every bone in her body was visible, and of course, had she known it, she was right. She placed one foot silently in front of the other and inched her way towards the dragon.

The dragon was enjoying himself, aware of the Princess with

the dagger on her belt, inching her way towards him. He was very patient as you get to be when you have lived for thousands of years. He waited, and he waited, and he waited.

Eloise was so close to the dragon she could feel its hot breath blasting out of its huge nostrils. If Eloise was in our world, which she isn't, because she lives in a land of swords, and dragons, and magic, but if she was, then the curled-up sleeping dragon would be about the size of three double decker London buses.

The eye that opened in front of her was about the size of a dustbin lid. It was huge with a dark black pupil, surrounded by a golden iris, that seemed to have living flames burning within it.

Eloise may have only been ten years old, but she had the heart and spirit of a mighty warrior. Straight away she knew the dragon could see her and she spoke in her clearest voice without a single bit of waver or tremor.

"Good evening Mighty Zoltan," she said, "I have come from afar to ask of you a special favour."

"Come my child," replied the dragon in a voice that was silken, and monstrous. "You are the Princess Eloise and you have come like an assassin in the night to kill me with your tiny dagger."

Eloise was completely taken aback by the dragon's perspicaciousness, still, she managed to maintain a clear unflustered expression.

"Oh no mighty Zoltan, I have heard of your great wisdom, and I come to beg a boon of you."

"Don't tax me child. One snap of my jaws and you will be undone. One hot breath, and your ashes will float before me like gossamer threads."

"Then why mighty Zoltan, am I not undone."

"Because you amuse me child, and to an extent, I almost admire you."

"Is it my beauty you admire great Lord?"

"No, my child, you know it is not. Do not push me with word

games child. They will not work. I admire your courage, cunning and most of all, your audacity."

"Shall we play chess my lord?"

"No, we shall not," replied the dragon, "but tell me child, what is this boon you would ask of me?"

"Oh, great Zoltan, I wish to feel your beating heart."

"All the better to kill me my dear."

"Oh no my Lord. They say a dragon's scales are the hardest thing in the realm. Even harder than diamonds."

"It is true my child," replied Zoltan, a little note of pride entering his voice. "What was the third of your spells my child?"

Eloise was again taken completely by surprise by the dragon's knowledge, but still managed to maintain her equanimity.

"It is a spell for courage my Lord, so that I wouldn't crumple up inside when faced with your magnificence," said Eloise, keeping her mind calm to hide her lie.

"Well my dear, you seem to have managed very well without it."

Eloise had been managing incredibly well. She had read all she could in Master Zagoop's library on the nature of dragons, and the one tiny detail, almost a throw away foot note, was the reference to a dragon's vanity. That was the chink in Zoltan's armour that Eloise was exploiting.

The King was in a flap. No one had seen Eloise or Rupert for days. The alarm had been raised by Feldon, who knew that protecting the Princess was more important than the embarrassment of been misled by her, or any retribution that might be coming his way.

The King just thought she was lost. It never occurred to him that his ten-year old daughter was off to save the realm. He had squads of guards and soldiers scouring the countryside, and forests. They were joined by most of the people from the towns and villages, for everyone loved the good King and his wonderful daughter.

The dragon held Eloise now with the powerful gaze of both his eyes. His tongue, larger than the greatest of boa constrictors, flicked in and out, little wisps of flame running along its length. As the dragon stretched, unfurled his coils, and spread out his mighty wings, Eloise was dwarfed, as a fish would dwarfed by a whale. The sharp teeth lining Zoltan's mouth, like rows of guards with spears, were massive, razor sharp and quite lethal.

"And what do you offer in return for this boon you ask of me?"

"I will serve you my Lord, as companion and amusement."

"You will serve me my child, as a tasty delicacy. My amusement will come in returning you, and your horse's charred bones, to that pompous father of yours."

"Oh no, my Lord Zoltan, replied Eloise smoothly, "for who in all these long ages has entertained you so, or had the presence of mind to talk with you as I do?"

The dragon allowed himself to have his vanity tickled and to be smooth talked against his better judgement.

"Okay my child, yes you have a deal. I will grant you your boon."

Eloise had to clamber over the dragon's legs to get towards its chest. It was like crossing huge hot metal plates, and although she wasn't burned, the palms of her hands were bright red from the heat, and sweat stung her eyes and soaked her clothing.

Eloise, startled by the dragon's knowledge of who she was, why she was here, and even what spells she had used, was trying to keep a tight guard on her mind so that the dragon wouldn't discover her design. All the while she was conversing with the dragon, trying to flatter him and appeal to his vanity.

"Oh mighty Zoltan, is it true as is whispered far and wide, that you have eaten more children than all other dragons together?"

"You are well informed my child."

"And is it true, your Magnificence, that in the old days philosophers and wizards came to you to learn of your mighty wisdom?"

"Yes child."

"And that on every occasion, you promised to teach them, but ate them instead."

"Oh yes, my child," replied Zoltan with a laugh so vigorous the mountain rumbled with the power of it, "but only after I had roasted them just the way I like them."

Eloise, clambering over the dragon's upraised chest, only just managed to hang on. Finally, she reached the part of his chest where great metallic plates thrummed with the steady massive beat of the dragon's heart.

Placing her palms on the plates, she felt the beat beneath her hands like her father's drums of war.

The dragon sensed the subtle change, the magic, like fine mist diffused through its being. Too late. Too late.

His whole body shocked as the tiny blade entered his heart.

"You lied, my child," screamed the mighty one.

"Yes, my Lord, the third spell penetrated your armour. Now my poisoned blade has undone you."

The dragon, full of rage and spite, stoked the fires of brimstone within, opened its massive jaws to roast the girl, and he lived no more. Crashing down to the floor of the cavern, he nearly accomplished by crushing, what he had failed to do with flame.

———

The King was pulled from the depths of a troubled sleep by the ringing of bells. The whole castle was alive with their crystal peals. Running out to the balcony, he stared down into the courtyard in disbelief.

There walking beside Rupert was Princess Eloise, garbed in her winter riding outfit, hair and cloth singed black by smoke and fire, holding aloft her mighty dagger. Behind Rupert, who was harnessed to a huge wain, sat the immense head of Zoltan, the silver dragon.

How the castle cheered.

CHECKERBOARD

SHE LOOKED at the square tiles on the wall and the checker board pattern on the floor, and they made her smile.

It had all started ironically, in a wood late at night. That was when they had met. They were there, right there, at the beginning.

She had been a student at film school. She had loved the movies, and growing up as a child had spent her private hours making shorts, putting on shows for her family, sending off her work to competitions and festivals, looking for a lucky break.

She had been able to choose a film school, and she had picked the best.

It was her friend Lisa who had seen the note on the student notice board. It was a common thing. There was always someone in the school with a project, looking for actors, technicians or just extras for a crowd.

This was a bunch of radicals shooting a horror flick in the woods. It was held to be ground breaking, the whole thing shot on hand held cams. Lots of jerky motion and raw realism.

That's where she had met Peter. He wasn't even in the movies.

He was just a friend of a friend, drafted in to run around the woods at night, getting gored up, having a crack.

They had met over a tea in polystyrene cups. Huddled together in the back of an old van, Billy the director, had borrowed for the night. It had been love at first sight.

That was twenty years ago. It had been twenty years of blissful marriage. She had gone on to be a successful filmmaker. Arty low budget films that drew respect in the industry, and won prizes at small film festivals. They often got included at Sundance and even Cannes back in '09.

Peter went on to develop a very successful Architects practice and she always thought they were the perfect couple.

It was ironic, because that film shot in the woods had gone on to be a world wide hit. It created a whole genre of grainy films shot on hand held cams.

Being an eminent if low key film-maker, she often was on judging committees for festivals. She watched a lot of movies, some of them inspired, occasionally dreadful, but mostly entertaining enough. After all it couldn't be any better than this. Not only did she do what she loved, making films, she got paid for watching them too. Life doesn't get any better.

She had her own private cinema in the basement of the house. She spent a lot of time down here watching the films they sent her. She loved the old days when she wound the spools of film into her projector, but now it was all digital.

She settled down with a lovely bottle of dry white wine, and pressed play.

This was the third film she had seen this week that used that slightly shaky hand held technique. She found it rather passé. It was not a technique she ever used, but she always felt a slight frisson of excitement when she thought back to that film in the woods long ago. It certainly hadn't hurt her career to be associated with a revolutionary block buster.

This film was shot from the perspective of an, as yet, unknown character. She recognised the location. A famous metro station in Paris with art on the walls. She had been there many times with Peter. At one time they had even had an apartment in that district of Paris.

Nothing much was happening, a few drunks on a bench on the opposite platform were raucously singing an old French ballad, popular ten years ago. Then that rumble and rush of air that preceded the arrival of a train.

The camera waited for the train to stop and the doors to open. She realised this take was just being shot on the fly. The camera took the audience onto a normal looking subway train and turned right. A punk with a scarlet quiff and a tartan jacket, sat vacantly in the first seat, lost in whatever music he was listening to, but as the camera focused a few rows back, her heart seemed to miss a beat in her chest, and her numb fingers let go of her wine glass, which unnoticed spilled its expensive contents on her carefully chosen fabrics.

In a daze she wandered up to the kitchen. She looked at the shining rack of Sabatier knives. Not quite right. She remembered that time in the woods. She remembered the feel of the hammer. Her hand seemed to reach for the meat tenderiser of its own volition.

Like a wraith she made her way up the thickly carpeted stairs. Numb to everything all she could see was Peter and Lisa side by side in the metro carriage. Lisa had aged well. Still a beautiful woman, her silken lips whispered silently into Peter's ear.

Pushing open the bedroom door, she silently entered the room. Peter, always so perfect. She stood by the bed watching the rise and fall of his chest, his handsome face.

Tightly holding the handle of the tenderiser behind her back she brushed her fingers lovingly on his cheek, whispering, "Peter, darling."

She watched his eyes open sleepily, smiling with love as he focused on her face.

She didn't even cry out as she brought the checker board pattern down onto his forehead with all her might. That was what she remembered. The regular squares embedded in his forehead.

By the time they had found her the tenderiser had done its work, the beautiful patterns obliterated. Still she appreciated the images. Focusing back on the tiles of her new home, she was looking forward to creating the juxtaposition of squares when she came to film it.

THE BUBBLE

THE BUBBLE slowly rose to the surface, carrying all the hopes and aspirations of a planet. It was the first.

The Boy carried his wooden sword proudly. He had walked many miles away from the area of the devastation. The cities lay in ruins. All vestiges of technology were gone. Hulking wrecks that once mighty, were now colossus collections of smashed steel and concrete. Roaming gangs like packs of rats swarmed the land devouring stragglers and lone travellers and yet still the Boy walked proud.

Corpses, mostly human, scattered the land, filling the air with that sweet smell of putrefaction and occasionally the Boy gagged with the stench of it, but still he carried on.

They stood blocking the road. Five men, faces burnt by radiation. Clothes blackened by filth and flame. What weapons they carried were simple but effective. The boy saw a hammer, some form of club or bat, chains, a rake, even the broken remains of a metal chair.

The threat was more a growl than language but the Boy understood. His sword was smooth, curved and carved from white oak from another land. It shone in the evening light from its lovingly polished wood.

Its first kiss was against the temple of the leader. There was a loud crack as the bone shattered but the Boy was in flight now. Spinning away from the falling body he brought the blade down in a cut on a shoulder, the wooden sword breaking rather than cutting the collar bone. A deflection inwards caught the line of the jaw and another dropped.

A roar behind him, caused him to pivot on the loose ground. A large wrench smashing down at his head. Moving subtly the Boy drifted like a wisp of smoke as the metal club crushed the empty air. Two small cuts of his blade almost like magic broke the descending arm at wrist and elbow and the wrench crashed down harmlessly hitting the ground almost simultaneously as the edge of the Boy's sword 'cut' through the throat, crushing the thorax with it's polished wooden edge.

A detached part of the Boy's consciousness remembered his Master and the moment he had presenting him with this beautiful blade that had become a part of him. A symbiotic partner that together weaved a life of love, motion and magic.

"Remember my Son, it is a sword. Whether finest folded steel or gift of the forest, the man and the blade become one.

The Boy continued on his journey. Behind him the scavengers remained, broken and quiet, and somewhere the bubble arrived at a surface, where it crossed into the emptiness and so, again, it began.

BAD CRAP CITY

BINKY BOO WAS PRETTY FED up of living in Bad Crap City. Police brutality, stinking sewers, moulding food not fit for pigs. Not that they had any pigs. Pigs had disappeared centuries ago. They had lasted for thousands of years, but couldn't compete with insects. However insects were processed and souped up, they still tasted like shit. The Romans used to keep pigs. They took up very little space and ate just about anything. Bet they wouldn't eat this muck though.

Binky ducked reflexively as a buzz fly shot past his head. Goddamn flies. Rumour had it some larky kid in a makeshift lab had mutated them. Whatever happened to good old computer hacking, and kicking the crap out of each other. Now every other kid's some kind of Frankenstein.

'I know,' Boo thought to the chip in his head, well not so much in his head, more a functional part of his head. 'Frankenstein was the creator, not the monster. That's what I said, ain't it?"

"The larky lad
Blew the life
From slime to the fly
Snipped his shit, graff knife"

"Best you can do"

"Got seventeen syllables."

"I've got a fishy one. Knock knock!"

"Who's there?"

"Hake."

"Haiku?"

"You're wasted."

"No, been clean for a week."

"No, wasted talent."

"I know, I'm just shitting with you."

SPICE

THE WATTLE BOTTLE Mega Gump Company was a rather over looked company that was based in a disused mill house in the West Riding of Yorkshire, England.

Wattle was the local name given to the spit of the lesser spotted horny toad that was endemic in this small part of Yorkshire. Who was the one who first imbibed this amphibian mucus is long forgotten in the mists of time. Did they kiss a toad, eat one for breakfast, squeeze it into a flavourless bug infested bowl of groats. What ever the chosen method they went on a trip of such mind bending proportions it made mescaline and LSD seem like junior aspirin, not known for its hallucinogenic properties, if any of these three drugs had been available in the year five hundred and twenty three.

Fortunately for posterity, this was the particular year that a wizard, lately of the court of a rather capable young king called Arthur, was travelling in Yorkshire with two knights, Cedric and Bertha, and a rather small fairy, who liked to travel disguised as a mouse, and spent a lot if time in the wizard's overcoat pocket.

This particular fairy, a young lady by the name of Bof, had arrived on Earth at a time thousands of years ago when Egypt was the largest spaceport this side of Andromeda. She had been stuck stranded there ever since, passing through human history, seeking out and befriending the odd bod creatives and weirdos of humanity like Leonardo Da Vinci in renaissance Italy, Minamoto No Yoritomo, the first Shogun in 12th century Japan, and Merlin the wizard of the court of Camelot in the small gap in England between the Romans and the Dark Ages.

Unfortunately, for future generations of pharmaceutical chemists and genetic engineers this particular species of horny toad with its spicy saliva, was very particular to a small bog near Wakefield and seemed immune to any form of cultivation, replication, or manufacture. In the same way that poison arrow tree frogs from the tropical Amazon forests created their toxins from their diet of insects, so this horny toad's gooey gob gestated from some particular dietary requirement only found in said bog.

Think spice of Arrakis and you will begin to realise the importance of Wattle to the functioning of the wider 'Verse. It was certainly a weird set of circumstances that brought Wattle to the attention of the pilots of hyperspace.

Merlin having drunk the local Inn dry of mead, and basically off his trolley, not that they had trolleys back then, was working on his art of talking to animals. The reason he isn't known as the Doctor Doolittle of the Dark Ages is that he wasn't terribly successful at it.

"And don't come back!" rang dully in Merlin's ears as his face crashed into the mud, fortunately cushioning his striking features from serious injury. The smell filling his nostrils from the mud that had squeezed in to them from the ordure that pregnated it, was like a dose of smelling salts. He pushed up with all his remaining strength to clear his face from the loathsome stench. Bof who had jumped from his pocket as the Innkeeper ejected him through the inn door, had metamorphosed into her normal form of a tiny fairy. She was flying before his face, her gossamer wings glistening in moonlight, and almost bent double in hysterical laughter.

"Come on Merlin, let's get you home."

Home was a large threadbare tent pitched on the edge of the bog. Bof lit her wand and guided the drunk wizard back to the camp, where he collapsed on a log next to the fire. It being a moonlit summer night Cedric and Bertha were still sat by the fire talking in subdued voices.

Merlin stared blankly at them, mud decorating his beard.

"What happened to him?" asked Bertha.

"The Landlord objected to Merlin telling his wife she was a salty looking witch."

"That would do it."

A suddenly rustling in the grass at the wizard's feet resulted in a hand shooting down with surprising velocity for a man in his cups. With a delighted smile he lifted the startled amphibian up into the air and studied him carefully in the firelight.

"Good evening Sir Toad," he addressed it.

The toad made no reply. Bringing it close to his face he repeated his message, this time in latin. Still no reply. Then he brought it so close, face to face, that his lips brushed against the toads.

"Put me down."

"Did you hear that," he cried out.

"What?" asked Bertha.

"The toad."

"The toad?"

"Yes," replied Merlin, " the toad told me to put him down."

"How much of that mead did you drink?" asked Cedric.

"All of it," Bof informed him.

"I tell you he spoke to me. Ask me a question."

"Ask you or the toad?"

"Me. Ask me a question."

"What's your favourite colour."

"No, a real question. A really hard one I wouldn't know the answer to."

"I've got one," said Bof.

"Shoot."

"What's the nearest spaceport to Earth?"

"What's a spaceport?" asked Bertha.

"Andromeda."

"What!" said Bof.

"Andromeda. I'm right aren't I. Ask me another."

"What's Andromeda?"

Bof was staring at Merlin.

"How long have I been on Earth?"

"Eight thousand three hundred and twenty two years, ninety days, and three hours forty five minutes. Wow, have you really."

"Yes," said Bof in a whisper, "Although I couldn't tell you that accurately. And can you do real magic and disappear."

"Yes," came the reply, and with that the wizard vanished.

OLD FRIENDS

BOTWINGA PITTO WAS an interesting character if interesting included a penchant for the melodramatic. At the moment Pitto was sat on his favourite bench on the edge of Napoleon's terrace overlooking the Piazza del Popolo with the still smoking remains of the Vatican in the background. The once beautiful shattered dome of Saint Peter's looking like a giant had smashed down the back of his teaspoon on the empty shell of his hard boiled egg.

There was a sudden silent pop, and Pitto was aware of a subtle smell of dried lavender and a feeling of substance or mass on the bench next to him. Turning he looked to see an elegant lady of senior years looking kindly into his eyes.

"Hello Botwinga," she greeted him.

"Hello Ann," he replied in his calm voice. "Would you be diverted by a bon bon, or maybe we could go down below for a coffee?"

"A bon bon would be nice, thank you."

The old lady with smile wrinkles around her beautiful eyes watched her old friend gently reach into the pocket of his frock coat and remove a white paper bag that rustled in the gentle breeze.

The lady placed a strong but delicate hand into the bag removing one of the sweets which she placed into her mouth before licking the icing sugar from her fingers.

"Delightful," she sighed.

Pitto watched the beautiful face of death as she sucked her treasure, her evident pleasure with its taste showing in the glow of her cheeks. He envied her her patience. He always tried as she, to allow the sweet to melt in the mouth, savouring its sugary flavour, first as the icing sugar dissolves, and then the solid mass held between the tongue and the roof of the mouth. He rarely accomplished this feat, but found himself chewing the nectarous ball, flecks of toffee like bits stuck in the gaps of his ageing teeth.

Still he held her eyes enjoying each moment as he had long ago being taught to do.

Finally, like the last few grains of sand slipping through an hour glass, the bon bon was no more. A silk handkerchief appeared in the lady's hand as if by magic, and she dabbed almost absent mindedly at her lip.

"It's not personal Botwinga."

"I know," he replied, all the time holding contact with the enchanting eyes."

A sudden pain erupted in his throat as the narrow blade slipped through the leathery and wrinkled skin, and the sparkling eyes glowed brighter for a brief moment before beginning to fade.

FILM NOIR

IGGI PIGGI WIGGI was crossing the street in old Gothenburg. It had been spending a couple of hours enjoying the quiet beautiful atmosphere of Ann's favourite bar in that city. The wonderful interior had calmed it, nursing a drink in the charming ambience, but the broad hadn't shown.

If you had spied Iggi slouching across the street you would have sworn it was Humphrey Bogart in a worn out mackintosh and scuffed Trilby hat because to all intent and purposes it was. Iggi had read all the Raymond Chandler books and watched all the John Huston films. His favourite was the Maltese Falcon. Really, the player he most identified with was always the Peter Lorre character. Low life double dealing slime ball. Those large bulging treacherous eyes. Casablanca was his tip top favourite, and that wasn't even a Chandler story. "You gotta help me Rick," he silently muttered as he crossed the bridge, dodging a tram on his way to the railway station.

Going to the premiers that was its thing. The Astoria Cinema in Greenwich village, or Mann's Chinese Theatre in Hollywood. It often went as the English actor, David Niven, because he wasn't the Premiere type. It gave Iggi a real kick to mix with the old stars, and if he was really lucky, seduce one of the beautiful starlets or leading ladies.

How they would scream if they saw its true form. The wet slimy face covered in little whistling suckers, them selves pustuled and knobbly like a rotting cheese. Iggi dreamed of doing it sometimes, but was too much the professional, and Iggi admitted to itself, too much the thespian to step out of its role.

With all the culture of this amazing world, Mozart's wood-wind concertos, Bellini's beautiful sculptures, all those Gothic cathedrals, it was the pulp fiction of Raymond Chandler and the movies of John Huston that really made its two hearts beat.

He could smell her, or at least her perfume.

"Oh Iggi," it heard whispered in its ear, "really," and then the simultaneous explosion of pain as the two blades slipped home into his waiting hearts, and the rumbling of the tram melted away.

HERE'S JOHNNY

THE BOY COULDN'T SLEEP. The clicking of the clock cracked in his hollow ears like Babe Ruth hitting pitches on Wrigley Field. Thwack. Thwack. Thwack.

What was that? A different sound. A sound of menace. Like a vibrating saw. Quiet at first, like a mosquito buzzing but growing in volume, intensity. The Boy's ears were beginning to scream with the crescendo of raw noise. He felt they must be bleeding with the fervor of the aural assault, and then suddenly there was silence. Absolute void. Had he gone deaf? Not even an echo.

His face felt hot like he was in the sun. There was no light, just the clawing darkness, and then the Boy felt the feet. Tiny ice cold feet like needle points, not sharp, not penetrating the skin of his face, but indenting it. Running down his forehead, past the damp corner of his eye, down his nose, and over his lips. Involuntarily he moved to swat away the intruder, but nothing happened. He had sent the signal, spontaneously reacted to the threat, but no hand had come to his rescue to brush away the intruder from his face, or strike it, crushing between flesh of palm and chin. The Boy's heart beat like a hammer in his chest and for the first time real panic ripped through him, and then he heard the voice.

"Here's Johnny!"

THE BRUSH

THE BRUSH FELT the texture of the paper. It wasn't smooth like glass but rough and uneven as it undulated below its bristles. Not bristles like the hard spikes driven into the wooden head of the broom of the yard, but delicate filigrees of hair like the velvety eyelashes of a bumble bee.

The brush felt the exchange. The black ink that soaked its silken fibres, dense and heavily concentrated at the tip, scarce and dilute by the shaft, not by water for the ground ink was uniform from the stone, but from lack of penetration as the brush had sucked it from the waiting pool.

With the single stroke of the artist's intent the brush swept across the waiting paper. The bamboo stem recreated in a single pass. The space, the light, from the top as rich and important as the deep black texture from the tip.

The brush was alive. It was the medium of love. The transmission of consciousness from the creator to the gifted. The vehicle of the journey connecting two beings of love.

As the beholder stared in wonder at the simple beauty feeling the texture of the Master's coexistence with their brush, a single tear rolled down his cheek and the journey was complete.

THE ADVENTURES OF BENJI MOUSE

THE MOUSE that was Benji stared into the huge eyes of the cat, and saw himself reflected back. Saw is a relative term. A fleeting part of him was aware of his mirror image, but he didn't stop for one millisecond. It was just a part of the mosaic of his awareness. That was why mice came apart. Their mind was their enemy. Their mind thought, stopped, analysed. You cannot be by thought. Benji Mouse was consciousness.

He could feel the beating of the cat's heart, the flicker of its whiskers. The smell of the fish it had eaten permeated, the very molecules of the air. The air that had been in the cat's lungs and were now in his sensitive little nose, his lungs, his very blood, was a part of him. Benji and the cat were not connected, they were one. A random thought flashed through the Storyteller, for he too was as one with the cat and the mouse.

At that moment, the cat and the mouse, turned to the Storyteller, and their eyes were as one. No fear, no violence, just love.

"We are consciousness," they said together.

"We are the grains of sand drifting on a Saharan dune."

"The moon beams dancing together on the edge of Jupiter."

"Is your consciousness joined like your particles?" asked the Storyteller.

"We don't know," replied Benji Mouse, "no one does."

The cat seemed to smile at the Storyteller. "Identity is an illusion. We have separation like two trees in a forest, nine planets in the solar system, a cat and a mouse. And yet we are one. "Is our consciousness our own or holistic? That doesn't matter. What matters is you."

"Me?"

"Yes, consciousness is you. The story you are telling is the magic of your existence. It has no importance to the whole. It is. When a wave travels on an ocean and breaks on a beach, it doesn't cease to exist, it never existed as a wave. That is just our perception. It's the sea. It was created by the wind, that shaped a tiny part of the seas surface for a while."

"And what of the wind that made the wave?"

"That doesn't exist either," answered the mouse, although it didn't matter which one spoke, they were as one. "The wind doesn't exist. It's just air moving around the planet because of a constant flux of pressure. The air, the sea, even the rocks of the earth are in motion, all part of the planet, which too is part of a whole."

"So I'm a wave."

"It's a nice metaphor," said the cat.

"Why are you the cat, and Benji Mouse has a name?"

"Because that is the way that you wrote us. If you trust consciousness, love it, bathe in it, it will guide you to write the story of your life. You are connected to your experiences and memories. They don't define you, but they may shape your story. Benji has been a character in your stories, so he has a name. I am no less important, name or no."

"You are more important," interjected Benji, "because consciousness is not about ego or identity it is about an awareness of being. Creativity and understanding. You humans have a great gift, yet in your arrogance as a species you assume you are unique. In the past, Men assumed they were superior to women, although they are two sides of the same coin. All of mankind's peoples assumed they were superior to their neighbours, but they were all men. Man thinks he is superior to elephants, whales, bees, and bacteria, but they are all life. Where does consciousness reside, we don't know, in the same way we will never know about faraway galaxies."

"Unless consciousness finds a way to close the gap," said the cat.

"Or consciousness allows you in to the conversation," said the Storyteller, who was an equal contributor to this one.

"Yes," added Benji, "we used to hug and smell, and read signals. We developed languages, smoke signals, writing, letters, telephones, it goes on."

"Yes, they are the tools and developments man has used to talk to each other. But what about talking to themselves, and to their life neighbours?" said the cat.

"But," interrupted the Storyteller, "consciousness isn't a tool, consciousness is."

"What, like God?" asked Benji.

"No, not like God. God is a simple answer to ignorance. Why am I here? How was the universe created? We know consciousness exists in man because we have it. We are aware of it. We have no idea whether it exists outside of man, but why not. Isn't that the whole province of religion and the corporations. God's chosen people licensed to abuse the planet because it was created for their use, their tribe, their socio-egoic group. We are more enlightened as a species. All humans have consciousness."

"Yes," said the cat, "and what about Elephants that you mentioned earlier. Strong family units. Sophisticated communication. Whales have brains the size of cars and a complex language humans don't understand, yet travels all around the oceans."

"And pigs, what about pigs," piped in Benji. "Ninety eight percent identical DNA to humans, very intelligent, can use a computer with a joy stick control, and yet instead of inviting them around to dinner, they are having them for dinner."

"Guys, guys," chided the Storyteller, we are getting way off base here."

"Is that a baseball metaphor," asked Benji.

"You know it is."

"What's baseball?" asked the cat playfully.

Because you have to be playful. Playful creates new thoughts, new opportunities. Life, the universe is in motion. Playful creates motion. Writing connects us to whatever is going on. If we trust consciousness, let it be the Storyteller of our story.

———

Benji mouse ran up the stairs, his umbrella under his arm, his top hat slightly askew on his head.

"Where are you off too?" asked Helen Mouse sweetly.

"Off on an adventure," called back Benji over his shoulder as he bounded over the top step, and rushed towards the front door, "want to come?"

"Yes please," said Helen breaking into a sprint up the stairs. "What do I need?"

"Well, that linen dress is just lovely, and your baseball boots of course. And you'll need binoculars, sandwiches, and some rope."

"Always need some rope," Helen muttered to herself as she raced to keep up with the departing mouse. She diverted through the kitchen door at the top of the stairs, and was quickly sawing sourdough with the serrated bread knife, and putting on lashings of butter, chocolate spread, and salami, before wrapping them in grease proof paper, and putting them in her satchel. "Don't go with out me, she shouted to Benji.

"Don't forget the sandwiches," floated back.

Helen grabbed her cardigan where it had been resting on the back of a rather nice but worn oak chair that she had restored for Benji, and painted a rather lovely eggshell pink, ran to the front door where she took an umbrella, a pair of old Zeiss binoculars, and a rather dashing purple silk cloche hat which she pulled tightly down to her ears, and ran out of the door, calling in her clear beautiful voice, "Wait for me Benji, wait for me."

She caught up with the adventurer just as he was casting off his little sailboat from the jetty on the river bank, nimbly jumping into the craft as it pulled away.

"Got the rope?" asked Benji.

"Of course," replied Helen with a smile, pointing to the coil of strong but lightweight climbing rope slung over her shoulder,"

"Excellent," said Benji with a happy grin that revealed his two chisel like front teeth that sparkled in the sunlight. "Grab that sheet, and tighten the sail, we're off to meet a dragon."

And simple as that with the sun glinting on the water, and bouncing off Benji's incisors, they were off.

The wind was howling and the horizontal rain was stinging Helen's cheeks, despite the hood of the bright yellow sou'wester that Benji had produced from the bilge of the boat, and the temporary shelter he had rigged up with a spare sail draped over the boom to make a rather cosy but damp tent. There were just polishing off the last of the chocolate and salami sandwiches.

"So when you say the dragon we are visiting is well read," asked Helen, "do you mean he is bright red, like a Welsh dragon, or that he has a magnificent library?"

"What makes you think that the dragon is a he?" replied Benji mouse, wiping a smear of chocolate from his whiskers with a crisply ironed, although slightly damp white handkerchief.

"Or maybe it's a hermaphrodite," added Helen, a girl and a boy, in the same pair of trousers."

"Dragons don't wear trousers."

"Why not," asked Helen, "Mice do?"

"Good point," acceded Benji, but dragons definitely don't.

And, to get back to your question, 'well read' as in has a well used magnificent library."

"How wonderful," said Helen, who loved reading books, and whose favourites included the complete works of Charles Dickens, Milly Molly Mandy, and the philosophy of Schopenhauer. "Will he or she allow us to browse their library?"

"Only if it doesn't roast or eat us first."

"Or both," pondered Helen, who was diligently licking the last of the chocolate spread from the creases of the grease proof paper.

The weather had improved. The river had become a lake or a loch or fjord, depending on where you were in the world, and the loch had become the sea. The sun was shining, the wind was blowing, and four socks flapped in the wind, tied to the jib sheet with bits of twine both drying and forming bright pennants as both Helen and Benji favoured colourful socks.

Benji was tacking against the wind which was always Helen's favourite part of sailing, as it gave the feeling of really flying through the water. Both she and Benji were on the edge of the boat with their furry feet and claws on the very edge as they hung on to the sheets and leant right over the side as the water rushed below them, to counter the lean of the boat in the wind,. It was very exciting.

In case you are wondering, and not yourself a sailor, the sheets aren't bed linen, brought on an adventure, they are the name that nautical types like Benji give to their ropes, perhaps to distinguish them from the coil of climbing rope that Benji told Helen to bring along.

"Are we there yet?"

Benji laughed.

"No, I was only half joking," said Helen joining in the laughter. "Is it far to the dragon's isle?"

Benji just smiled. His left hand was holding the sheet and the wind pulled at his whiskers, fur, and jacket, making a loud vibrating sound. His top hat was stashed safely in the boat and his little ears rippled in the breeze. With his other hand he took a carved ebony pipe from his jacket pocket, placed it in his mouth, where he bit down on the stem to keep it in place, patted down the tobacco with his thumb, then reached in to the fob pocket of a bright paisley waistcoat where he withdrew instead of a watch on a chain, a shiny gold lighter on a chain. Helen, whose sense of smell was very acute, could smell the petrol in the lighter, and wrinkled her nose in disgust. Oblivious of the wind whipping them as they raced along, Benji turned his head so the pipe was in the lee of the wind, flicked the lighter with his thumb, and sucked contentedly as he drew the flame into the bowl making the tobacco smoulder, blowing out a plume of pungent smoke from the side of his mouth which followed their little boat like a vapour trail.

"Filthy habit," shouted Helen over the noise of the wind, and although she wouldn't admit it to the mouse, she did rather enjoy the aromatic smell of his tobacco.

Whereas some dragons in the world are the size of several London buses, and in the very big ones that's just the size of their head, Matilda was about the size of a Saint Bernard dog. What she lost in absolute size she made up for in her fiercesome appearance as she was well red in both senses of the word.

Her scaly skin was bright scarlet with little purple veins of hue that ran between the scales like little traces of cold fire. The hot fire flickered from her long slender mouth, lined with great scything razor sharp teeth, and she had the most beautiful almond eyes Helen thought, although they actually glowed luminously in a most disconcerting way.

Of course on a comparative scale from Benji mouse to Matilda dragon, the size differential was enormous. Benji had warned

Helen on their approach to the isle to be very careful she wasn't accidentally squashed.

Currently they were sitting in Matilda's beautiful library. Helen had never seen so many books, all bound in beautiful leather or wood, and embossed with gold and silver writing. Helen had grasped immediately, and rather disappointedly, that she wouldn't be reading any of Matilda's books, as compared to her and Benji, each one was about the size of Benji's shed where he had a little workshop outside his burrow. Perhaps they could ask Matilda to read to them. A wisp of flame and green smoke escaped from her mouth, violently contrasting with her scarlet scales, and Helen wondered that it was a surprise that all these beautiful books hadn't been accidentally burned away long ago. With a start, Helen realised she had been drifting, and had missed something.

"Pardon," she said.

"Would you like some tea dear?" repeated Matilda, "Benji always likes my Darjeeling."

And so they all sat down for tea.

———

What Helen hadn't understood about books in a Dragon's library was that reading them was like living them.

"But that is always how I read books," replied Helen to Benji, when he had supplied this information over a breakfast of scrambled eggs on toast with crispy bacon and mushrooms.

"You are missing the point, my dear," said Benji. "I know when you read a normal book, that is maybe an extraordinary book like 'The Lion, the Witch, and the Wardrobe,' but one that you read on paper with your eyes, your powerful imagination transports you to the author's world, and it is as if you are there."

"And, in a dragon's book?" asked Helen.

"In a dragons's book, my dear, you really are there."

"What so if, for example, I'm balancing on a rope bridge,

crossing a chasm of burning fire, fighting a retreating battle against a vampire cat, and singing the hallelujah chorus, and the cat catches me with a blunt blow to the head with the flat of its sword, and my feet lose their grip on the rope, and I topple sideways and fall towards the fiery heat, I'm toast?"

"Burnt to a cinder," said Benji before putting his last piece of bacon from his fork to his mouth, "crisper than this bacon."

"Gosh," said Helen, and quietly sipped her tea.

Benji mouse kissed the ground in gratitude. They had survived. It was only earlier that they had met the rabbit. The mad mad rabbit.

Most rabbits of Benji's acquaintance had been natural rabbits. When he said natural, he meant like him and Helen. Rabbits or mice of the land.

They might wear fine silk or coarse cloth waistcoats and trousers, or print cotton dresses, but underneath they had brown fur and black eyes. The mad rabbit had pure white fur and eyes that were evil, and red, and Helen swore, they glowed in the dark.

It had been in the library that they had first encountered the rabbit. Initially Benji had taken him for another guest, but it was Helen that knew him as an interloper,

"Hello little mices," it whispered in a voice both like acid, and like gravel grinding, or avalanches rumbling in the mountains. "Are you my breakfast?"

"Don't be ridiculous," replied Helen sharply, "do we look like porridge or scrambled eggs?"

"You look like it to me," said the rabbit in his gravelly voice, for Benji was sure it was a he. "You would go well with some worms."

"My name is Helen Mouse," said Helen in her strident voice, "and I want you to know I don't take any nonsense from the likes of you." As she said this she glared straight into the rabid red eyes of the rabbit, no sign of fear at all.

"And I am The White Rabbit, a psychotic, if I say so myself, pan dimensional being from another galaxy. How do you do?"

'Well at least it's polite,' thought Benji, no longer sure whether it was a he, she, or it.

"I'm very well thank you," replied Helen graciously, "or I was until meeting you,"

"Steady madam," the rabbit growled like a dying badger, "manners maketh creature."

"But what kind of creature are you?"

"A very mean one," replied The White Rabbit with a smile that broadened into a sickly grin, before widening into a void-like maw of jagged sharp teeth.

"Run," cried Benji, and without a look back the two mice turned tail and fled out of the library.

Benji and Helen had wandered into an unusual rock formation known locally as the dragon's nostril. The rock itself seemed warm and glowed a slightly red colour which gave the two mice enough light to see by.

"Where do you think we are?" asked Helen.

"Absolutely no idea," admitted Benji. "These red rocks give me the creeps," which of course is the last thing that Helen wanted to hear.

Benji had been leading the way down the strange passage. They had raced out of the library away from The White Rabbit and got hopelessly lost. During the last few minutes the passage seemed to be getting hotter and brighter. The strange rock seemed to be marbled with a shiny red obsidian and this was the source of the eerie glow. Pausing to take a large handkerchief from his breast pocket to mop his brow, Benji caught sight of

Helen behind him with a steely look in her eye and a rather large duelling pistol held comfortably in both hands.

"Wherever did that come from," he asked in a level voice, as if enquiring about a new hat.

"It was Daddy's," she replied, "he brought it back from his adventures in the Emerald Mountains."

"The Wolf Wars," said Benji in a respectful tone, "I didn't know any mice had returned alive."

"He never spoke about it."

"And you've had it all this time."

"A girl should never leave home without her gun," replied Helen with a smile.

Suddenly the passage was filled with a rumbling sound like giants' teeth grinding together. The very rock around them and under their feet seemed to vibrate.

"Uh oh," said Benji, and at that moment the passage before them opened up in to a seemingly endless cavern with a huge pair of eyes filling the darkness.

"Watch out," cried a voice from behind him, followed by the crack of Helen's pistol and then the world was plunged into darkness.

"You know the giant was going to eat the man?" rumbled the voice in the dark.

"You're not going to eat us," Helen sang in her soprano voice, "you're just messing with us."

"Oh ho ho," grumbled the reply, "you really THINK SO?"

The last two words were shouted like explosions in a quarry, and echoed deafeningly in the darkness.

"I dooooo," Helen continued to sing, and with a deft movement unseen by Benji, she opened the clasp on her bag, reaching confidently inside, and whipped out her own zippo lighter, which she clicked with her thumb, all in one flowing movement.

Bright light erupted from the tiny flame, and the pupils of the giant eyes constricted to tiny pinholes, framed as they were by the huge face of their host, Matilda, the dragon.

"You were right," she said, "I was only messing with you. Would you like some tea?" And she indicated with a well manicured claw to a pot of tea and slices of apple cake on a mahogany table.

"So what was that all about?" asked Helen.

"What?" replied Benji.

"This whole malarkey. A huge introduction about consciousness, and then a tale about a visit to a dragon."

"Well, you'd better ask the storyteller."

"Oh, he doesn't know. He hasn't got a clue. It's all just spontaneous outpouring. There's no plan, it just vomits out."

"Sometimes there's a plan," said the storyteller.

"Rubbish," replied Helen. "You just start writing and out it comes. It doesn't matter what you write. It's the writing that's important."

"The act of creativity," added Benji, "connecting to the core."

"Yes," continued Helen, "every moment spent in Fantasia is a moment connected to your true self. Whether it's writing stories, or poetry, playing avant garde jazz on your cello, or drawing a picture, you are on a journey with you, and it's beautiful."

"Sounds like a lot of nonsense," said the cat, and with a flick of its paw and a gulp, he swallowed them whole.

THE LEAVES

MILLICENT GREEN READ the leaves that created an unseen pattern in the china cup. It made no difference whether it was a cup, mug or polystyrene beaker, the deposit of leaves arranged like scattered stars in an evening sky told their story.

Well, not their story for the leaves themselves had no future other than the story of all things, the transformation from one energy state to another. No, the leaves told the future story of the person who had drunk the tea.

For Millicent had the gift. She had inherited it from her mother, and her mother before her, going back into the mists of time. It was said within this female line, a warning of things gone by, and maybe of things to come again, that her Great Great Great Grandmother had been burned as a witch. Sometimes in her dreams Millicent was aware of the flames and the screaming.

"Will I meet a tall dark stranger?"

Millicent looked not at the leaves but at the young smartly dressed woman before her. Professional she guessed, maybe a lawyer or a doctor. Expensive but subtle couture dress. A handbag on the floor by her chair that would pay for a new car for Millicent.

"I wonder if there has been a mistake," she said coldly. "It says quite clearly in my advertisement, no time wasters."

The young woman looked slightly abashed. She reddened, and Millicent wondered if she had misread her from her deportment and presentation.

"I'm sorry," she said earnestly, "I meant no disrespect."

"Is this a birthday treat, or a dare?" Millicent asked.

"No, no, not at all. I believe. I'm just nervous of what you might say. I was being amusing."

The look in Millicent's eyes softened and the young lady visibly relaxed.

"Then let's continue shall we?"

Millicent reached across and took the now empty cup staring into its revealing depths.

"What's the matter, what do you see?"

"I'm sorry, my dear, there seems to be a mistake." Millicent stammered. "I must be poorly, the leaves aren't speaking to me."

"You're lying," said the young woman, "You looked into my cup and went white as a sheet."

"There's no need to be rude my dear," said Millicent, "I looked into your cup and nothing was there. Of course I will refund your fee. I stand by my guarantee."

The young lady had looked slightly mollified by the return of her fee although Millicent knew that she would have no benefit from it. As she watched her front door close behind her she closed her eyes and waited for the screeching of brakes and the terribly loud bang of a car hitting a body.

VIGILANTE

MATT FELT the muscles in his arms twitching, then screaming. It had started again.

The baseball bat swung at his head, but he had so much time to react, he felt like a house fly. His left hand stopped the bat with a crack like thunder, and his right fist drove into the villain's head so hard, the face wetly crumpled, before the head left the body and ricocheted off the alley wall.

Matt was what they called in the comics a super hero. His costume had been sewn with precision by his mum, so he was looking cool.

He had been sat at home watching telly when he got the feeling. He likened it to a spider sense. He knew when and where people were in trouble. He made some excuse to his mum about the Internet and sidled upstairs, and even as he went his body was transforming. He became like the Incredible Hulk, only slimmer, smaller, less monochrome, and better looking. He took his costume out of the wardrobe and quickly got changed.

The woman's scream was full of fear. She smelled the fetid breath and felt the weight of her attacker. Suddenly the weight was released and a new smell, that of fresh arterial blood, filled her nostrils. A hand reached out of the darkness and with a kind word she was helped to her feet.

The air buzzed with the hum of radios, and the flashing blue lights were giving her a headache. For the fifth time she tried to tell her story to the hard-bitten cop.

Rattigan spat into his radio, "Goddamn vigilante again." This was the third case this week and they seemed to be accelerating. He put a large pinch of Old Holborn on the paper, evened it out, and expertly rolled a cigarette, licking the gum to fasten it down. Sucking the pungent smoke into his ravaged lungs he sighed to his partner and repeated, "Goddamned vigilante."

Matt loved his comics. Judge Dredd was his favourite. "I am the law," rang through his very being, so when his transformations first began, he knew what was happening, as if he had been expecting it his whole life, and he knew what he had to do. "With great power comes great responsibility," and for Matt, the borders between fantasy and reality had always been blurred.

The Pimp felt his rib cage give way. The nutter in the fancy dress suit had hit him so hard it was like being struck by a train, or so he imagined as his legs buckled, and blood-stained vomit spewed down his suit. He loved that suit, a dark grey vintage Armani, left by a punter scammed by one of the girls, and everyone said how sharp it was. About as sharp as the fractured rib that had perforated his liver causing the internal bleeding that was draining the life out of him.

Matt felt great with each rescue, or mission, as he liked to call them. It was as if the essence of the villains fed his super-ness, like a street vampire sucking the life force out of its victims. He felt great, and let's face it he was a goddamn hero.

Rattigan hawked up a mouthful of nicotine stained phlegm and spat at the feet of the reporter. "Goddamn vigilante," he repeated for the dozenth time.

The Journo was no rookie. He knew Rattigan's reputation, and treated him with a mixture of contempt and respect. "Rattled because he's doing your job," he taunted, and straight away regretted it as Rattigan gave him the eye.

"Piss off punk," Rattigan snarled and the Journo backed off a step.

From out of the darkness, a fist smashed like a striking snake into Rattigan's head, knocking him flat. His ear split and exploded with blood from the force of the punch.

Matt sidled into the kitchen and handed his blood-stained costume to his Mum to put in the wash.

"Cup of tea, love?" she asked as she leant over to peck him on the cheek. "Busy night?"

———

Betsy screamed with joy and skittered down the corridor to the nurse's station. The abandoned room beeped loudly with the alarm on the life support machine.

Consciousness, when it came, was clear and sudden. Rattigan had lain in a coma from massive head trauma for six long weeks, but now, he felt great.

The head nurse ran into Rattigan's room to find him standing naked but for his hospital gown, buttocks exposed to all the world, rolling his Old Holborn tobacco, whilst staring out the window. Feeling her legs buckle slightly, her starchy years of training saved her as she told him, "Put that cigarette out right now, Mister Rattigan."

The last thing Rattigan remembered was talking to that goddamn Journo, and then, suddenly, he was here. Betsy, through joyous sobs, filled him in. Punched by a masked vigilante, he had suffered extensive brain injury, and now, a miracle.

Rattigan didn't know what all the fuss was about, he felt great! In fact, it was as if the world had been polished. His vision was fantastic, and he could hear a faint conversation at the nurse's station, wonder mixed with fear,

"But it's impossible…"

"No one could recover from such an injury…"

Rattigan had had enough. "Stop whining," he snapped at Betsy, "and get me some goddamn clothes."

The Journo was nervous. For the last six weeks he had been the man of the moment. On the scene, his front-page story was rumoured to be up for the Pulitzer. Now, summoned to Rattigan's office, he pushed the door open.

"Not so goddamned cocksure now," Rattigan growled between drawn lips, precariously balancing his rollup. He was back on the case and the fact that he had suddenly become the Vigilante's latest victim was baffling him. However, that had been six weeks ago. Since then there had been another twenty-three deaths. Rattigan was the only victim to have survived.

To the young Journo, Rattigan was now as big a story as the Vigilante. According to the hospital, Rattigan had made a complete recovery. "A Medical Miracle?" He was already playing with his headline.

Seeing that the Journo was distracted, Rattigan squeezed his shot glass of bourbon in irritation, and it exploded in a hail of fine glass shards. Rattigan, as surprised as the Journo, but not showing it, threw the remains into the trash. The Journo inwardly gulped, the cop's hand wasn't even bleeding.

"Breakfast!"

Matt heard his Mum yelling up the stairs and went down for his breakfast. Glancing at the newspaper on the table, he spat his tea out in amazement. There was a picture of that cop, what's his name, Rattigan, walking out of the hospital looking right as rain. Recovering his composure, Matt put jam on his toast and gazed at his suit, freshly ironed and hanging on the clothes horse.

Rattigan tilted his hat forward and pulled his collar up as he stepped out of the station back door into the alley and pouring rain. He could feel something was happening, didn't know what, didn't care. "Bring it on you goddamn pansies," he muttered.

Without thought he spun around, his left arm moving up and back, catching the punch on its inward flight, gliding it past his head as his right fist came around in the same motion, and connected with the jaw of the guy in the red costume. Rattigan exulted. Never had he moved so fast or hit so hard. His assailant's head and body shot sideways into the wall of the narrow alley and brick fragments exploded outwards as the wall smashed with thunderous applause.

Rattigan was just a bit too cocky, because next it was his turn to bounce off the other alley wall. The blow to his ribcage should have shattered it, but instead the punch sent him rocketing within the confined space.

Light from the open station door flooded down the alley as the open-mouthed Captains and clerks stood in the rain watching the two titans hammer each other, doing little damage, except to the architecture.

Matt was beginning to panic. What the hell was going on? He had crept silently up on the cop, to finish the job for good, when all hell had broken loose. Suddenly the cop was as strong as he was! Matt was getting tired. He wished he'd had an extra slice of toast for breakfast this morning. With an unexpected twist, he broke off, made a run for it, and jumped the six-foot iron gate at the end of the alley as he made his escape.

Rattigan watched him go. Goddamn Vigilante, that was two suits he had ruined. Picking his crumpled hat up from the side walk he started rolling a cigarette and shuffled back to the station. Goddamn, he needed a drink.

———

As the slugs hit his chest, Rattigan staggered. A good grouping, he would think later when he examined the bruising with Betsy. He wasn't wearing a vest. Didn't need a vest. Why waste the budget on a SWAT team, when all they had to do was send in Rattigan. Goddamn Pinkos.

The Pinko was sat at the bar. His face was a nest of activity, full of ticks and grimaces, rodent features, oddly disturbing.

The Girl put the coffee in front of the Pinko and skittered back to the other end of the counter. The Pinko gave her a gap-toothed leer and slurped his coffee from the saucer. He'd seen it done in an old movie and thought he was the height of cool.

"Give me the goddamn money!"

The round end of the revolver filled the Girl's vision, terrifying her with its cold metal precision.

Two almighty crashes, so close together only an audio dilettante could have told them apart, heralded the entrance of a hard-bitten cop, trench coat flowing in the wake of his passing, hat rakishly balanced on his head, and a masked guy in the red fancy dress costume that looked like his mum had made it.

Matt, having the slight edge in super hero experience, got there first and slammed the Pinko's head so hard into the counter a horizontal wave of blood shot out in all directions as if he'd slammed a ketchupped burger with the grill pan.

"Goddamn Vigilante," drawled Rattigan as he grabbed his nemesis and rocketed him into the juke box which exploded in a flash of smoke and flames, still managing to beat out Marvin Gaye's old tune, 'I heard it through the grapevine.'

"And, another thing," yelled the Captain to Rattigan. "How in hell's name is the department going to pay for the damage?"

Rattigan just looked down at his shoes and rolled a cigarette. You could be as tough as you like and a super hero, but no one wanted a grilling from the Captain.

"And another thing," the Captain shouted, his face beginning to blotch purple, "not only did you trash the place, the goddamn vigilante got away, and the Girl's family is suing the department for a lifetime's care at the local nut ward."

Betsy was in a bit of a daze. She was ironing Rattigan's shirt in front of the TV and she was sure she could smell burning. She looked down and screamed at the sight of the iron smoothing out the back of her hand. The smell was the blackened fine hairs. She ran to the faucet and shoved her hand under the cold tap. She knew how to treat a burn, she knew first aid. It must be the shock, but there was no pain, in fact, although the hair had burned away, her skin wasn't even red. Betsy had her moments, and cautiously went back to the ironing board, picked up the iron. Her heart beat excitedly with anticipation, as she gently touched the hot iron to her palm.

The Journo got the call from his Editor. Some perve predator, well known in the seedier parts of town, was in the local hospital with multiple fractures in both his arms and his legs. Although his head was in plaster and his jaw wired together, the Journo heard him silently rattle, "It was a broad, a goddamn beautiful broad."

Betsy was fed up. When was that goddamn Rattigan going to come and get her out?

The duty sergeant reached his hand through the bars and lit the cigarette held firmly in Betsy's bright red lips.

They were treating her like a goddamn criminal when she had been fighting for justice, the Metropolitan way. Where was that goddamn boyfriend of hers?

Rattigan was at his wits end. Bad enough dealing with the goddamn Vigilante, now Betsy had gone super, and made mincemeat of some perve from the sticks.

She would have got away with it too, but apparently was so angry at laddering her stockings, she kept smashing the Perve's face into the edge of the sidewalk.

"About goddamn time," Betsy purred as she flicked her lipstick coated butt into the ashtray.

There was an edge to Betsy that Rattigan hadn't seen before, and he wasn't sure he liked it. What in hell's name was going on? He knew one thing for certain, he was going to have to find somewhere to send his shirts.

THE OLD MAN

THE POSTMAN PUSHED the envelope through the letter box, announced by a clump sound as it snapped shut behind, drowning out the softer sound as the letter fell to the linoleum floor.

Henry Spalding-Smith shuffled down the empty corridor, his worn woollen slippers muffling his footfall on the cold plastic floor except for the slight dragging sound of his gammy right leg. He always told his grandson, nice lad, that it was the result of a small stroke when he was near retirement at the ministry, but in truth it was the result of being wounded in Africa back in the seventies. He had been serving in a mercenary unit in Angola, one of many fighting the government's secret wars serving the interests of the Tobacco companies.

He took the letter from the floor and made his way back to the kitchen where it rested on the table top staring up at him as he poured a cup of tea from the pot and lit a Woodbine cigarette from an almost empty packet. They were hard to come by these days. Coffin nails they used to call them in his Grandfather's day. He sucked the raw smoke into his ancient lungs, coughing slightly, taking a pristine white handkerchief from his dressing gown pocket and hawking a green gob of mucus into its welcoming depths.

Major H Spalding-Smith was typed, with a typewriter, not printed, the capital S slightly italic from being offset, on the rectangular manilla envelope, followed by his address at a mews house in Chelsea, London.

Taking a sip of Ceylon tea from the worn bone china cup, he returned it to its saucer, and flicking ash into an empty tobacco tin on the checked formica table cloth, he put the cigarette between his lips where he drew on its pungent wares as smoke escaped, increasing the fog-like atmosphere of the kitchen.

A knife appeared as if from nowhere in his hand, a simple ebony handle and sharply curved double blade, and Henry picked up the envelope and with a fluid action slit it open and withdrew the folded piece of paper, and unfolding it, placed it on the table beside the now empty envelope. Three words had been typed in capital letters.

THEY ARE COMING.

THE LAUGHING MAN

THE LAUGHING man coughed with embarrassment as he realised his joke wasn't funny.

The quiet man minding his own business, calming put down his knife and fork, pulled his napkin that he had been using as a bib from where it had been tightly inserted into his collar, dabbed his lips to remove a trace of gravy, and stood up. Before anyone realised what was happening, he stepped up towards the comedian, who had a flustered look as the approaching man with the soft face, crumpled bowler hat, and worn overcoat, pulled something gently from his coat pocket, and swiped his hand in an arc across the entertainer's throat. A bright red spray of blood erupted like a fountain jet from a squeezed hose, right over the brim of the man's hat and into the faces of the aghast diners in the tables behind. For a moment there was a pregnant silence and then several women screamed in broken harmony.

A clear voice from a little old lady in a blue velvet dress said, "They always were a tough crowd at the Apollo."

ELOISE AND THE GRUMBLY GHOST

ELOISE WAS EXPLORING the dungeons of the castle. She loved tiptoeing through the pitch-black corridors in the outer reaches of the east dungeon. That was the place where the prisoners were kept in the olden days. It was whispered throughout the castle that Alonzo the Bad, the King's Great-Great-Grandfather, used to keep his prisoners here, and the whispers also said that, Alonzo the Bad wasn't very nice.

None of the castle children, the children of the soldiers, the nobles, and the servants, would go into that part of the castle, but for Eloise, that was even more reason to go there. She loved the peace and quiet of the desolate passages.

There was nothing more Eloise liked than to take a good book, sit on an old box with a candle and read a great story.

"The little girl sat in front of the light box, eating wafer thin potato slices cooked in horrid oil, whilst watching magic pictures on the screen of light." It was too horrifying, and Eloise slammed her book shut. What a nightmare!

"I was enjoying that," grumbled a voice behind her. Eloise almost jumped out of her skin.

"Who said that," she said bravely, whipping around to face the voice, holding the candle up to light the empty corridor.

"Only Me," came the same voice from behind her.

Eloise was wise and brave and straight away she could see this game could continue indefinitely, so instead she blew out her candle, and in her strongest voice asked, "And who is Me?"

"I am Me." And in front of Eloise there materialised the grumpiest and saddest face she had ever seen.

"Nice to meet you," replied Eloise politely, "and now that we have been introduced, can you tell me please what you are doing here, and whatever is the matter with you?"

The King was a very wise man. He needed to be to rule the Land in a just and fair way. At the moment he had a rather concerned look on his face.

"A ghost?"

"Yes Papa, and he's all alone, and he doesn't know he's died."

"Have you been getting enough sleep my child?"

"Papa," said Eloise sharply, "it's the middle of the day. I'm not silly, or asleep or dreaming. I met a ghost and he needs my help. He doesn't know he is dead and he's very sad. How can I help him please?"

The King was surprised at the sharp angry tone in his daughter's voice. It reminded him of her Mother. When you are a King most people tend to tip toe around you, being on their best behaviour. Eloise was only eleven years old now, and she was talking to him in the same way as one of his advisors. He was both proud and annoyed, at the same time. Proud of what a grown up young girl she was becoming, and annoyed that she was bothering him with this nonsense, when he was so busy with affairs of State.

Eloise was back in her bedroom. She was angry and disappointed, both because her Father had dismissed her and not taken her seriously, but also because she had thought the King could advise her on how to help Me.

Eloise decided to go and see her best friend, Rupert. She changed into her riding clothes, grabbed her hard hat and her sword, and wound her way down through the castle's secret and quiet ways, through the warm kitchen with its delicious smells, and outside towards the stables. She always took her sword when she left the castle, especially after her adventure with the Silver Dragon.

Eloise always had a few biscuits in her pockets to give to Rupert, her beautiful white stallion. In truth, Rupert didn't belong to her, he was a free spirit. A beautiful creature who chose to share his existence with Eloise, and before that with Jagerd, the King's captain, who had rescued Rupert from the great wolf beast, whose head now decorated Eloise's bedroom wall.

Rupert and Eloise went for a wonderful ride through the forest together, cantering through the trees, whilst Eloise told Rupert all about Me, and his sadness.

Unfortunately, being a horse, Rupert wasn't able to give Eloise any actual advice, and she decided to bring it up with Jagerd, when she went for weapons training.

"How did you cut it off?"

"What?" asked Eloise politely.

"The dragon's head of course."

Since his friendship with Eloise, Me had become more confident in himself, so instead of wandering lost up and down the dungeon passages, he had been exploring all over the castle.

As Eloise had explained to Me, "That is one of your many advantages. You can pass through walls, and be invisible." Eloise was finding it difficult to teach Me the advantages of being a ghost, when he didn't grasp that he was a ghost, or even that he wasn't actually alive at all!

Me's favourite place was the kitchen, which was warm and cosy. He liked to sit in the arm chair by the fire, enjoying the hustle and bustle. It was a little microcosm of the whole world, and Me loved it.

This was where he had heard the story of Eloise killing the dragon, cutting off its head, and bringing it back to the castle, bravely pulled on a makeshift bier, by Rupert.

Eloise had always been brought up to be honest and truthful, and this to an extent, overrode her natural tendency for modesty.

"It is true that I killed Zoltan, The Silver Dragon, who was terrorising our land," she said in a serious tone. "I went with Rupert to Zoltan's mountain lair, found my way in to the heart of the mountain, and tricked him, so I could stab him through the heart."

Me was enthralled hearing the story at first hand like this.

"So, what happened next?"

"I set off for home. It's a long way, and I had missed lunch, dinner, and supper!"

"So, you didn't cut his head off and drag it back with you, like everyone says?"

Eloise appraised Me with a sympathetic eye. She was a lucky girl, a princess with tutors, and mentors, who had taught her about the world. Me was a ghost living in a dungeon. When he was alive, he probably hadn't had much experience of life either. At that moment Eloise had a clear thought about how lucky she was.

"Do you know what an Elephant is?"

"No."

"Well it's really big. Twice as tall as the tallest man, with a great big trunk, and huge flappy ears."

"What's a trunk?"

"A huge long nose like a giant snake, that's clever and sensitive at its end, and can pick up things, and tickles your hand when you give it a biscuit."

Me was amazed. He couldn't imagine this monster at all.

"Oh, it's not a monster," said Eloise sagaciously. "They live in the wild like horses do, but they are very intelligent. Just like Rupert," she said proudly, "and sometimes, they share our lives with us."

In fact, Eloise knew that sometimes, in faraway places, some animals weren't treated very well, but in her Father's kingdom, which he ruled wisely, everyone, and everything was treated with respect. However she didn't want to confuse Me. Eloise realised that she had become his mentor, and it brought a happy smile to her face.

"And what about the elephant?" asked Me, getting back to the point.

"Yes, well they are really big, and the dragon's head was as big as an elephant, and its neck was like the trunk of an ancient tree, and I couldn't possible have cut through it with my little sword."

"So, how did you cut it off?"

"I didn't," said Eloise, trying very hard to be patient, and keep out the note of exasperation that was trying to make itself heard. "On my way back from Zoltan's mountain I came across a company of the King's Guard who had been sent out to look for me. It was they, under the leadership of Gordon, Captain of the Guard, who went back to the mountain, chopped off the dragon's head and mounted it on a wooden bier."

"But it was you and Rupert that brought it back to the castle."

"Yes," replied Eloise, quite proud of her achievement.

Forgetting he was a ghost, Me jumped up to give Eloise a hug, and passed right through her.

"What was it like?" asked Jagerd, who was a party to her secret, the next day at training.

Like a sparkle or a tingle, like an energy," she replied.

"Then you are a very lucky girl."

And deep inside, Eloise knew that she was.

There comes a time in everyone's life when they need to step out of the comfort of the familiar. Today it was Me's turn.

"What do you mean, leave the castle?"

"Not for good," reassured Eloise, "we will start with a visit to Rupert."

"Who's Rupert?"

"Rupert is my best friend?"

"Aren't I your best friend?"

Eloise could see it was going to be a difficult day. "Didn't you ever leave the castle when you were alive?"

"What do you mean alive?"

Eloise sighed. She had forgotten that Me didn't know that he was a ghost, and therefore had died, and so wasn't alive. She decided to change tack.

"Haven't you ever left the castle before?"

"Oh no," replied Me, "why would I do that? Until I met you, I spent all my time walking around here and playing games."

"What sort of games?"

"You know, all the usual ones, chase the spider, count the cobbles, talk to the rats, all those games."

"Did they ever talk back?"

"The rats? No, they never did. Very unfriendly I always thought."

His voice, Eloise thought, was a lot less grumbly than it used to be.

"So, who taught you to read," Eloise asked, remembering the first time they met. "Was it your Mummy?"

"What's a Mummy?"

After a long silence, a quiet voice asked Eloise, "Why have you got your sad wet face again."

"And," continued Eloise, "he doesn't even know what a Mummy is, let alone remember his own."

Eloise was sat on an old tree stump in a sunny glade talking to Rupert. It was one of her favourite places.

Like Me's rat friends, Rupert never actually talked back, and realising their connection, she felt a new affinity with Me. Being a Princess meant that real friends were quite hard to come by.

———

Eloise and Me tiptoed down the passageway. Her warrior training had taught her to move without a sound, and Me, being a ghost and therefore, incorporeal, was as silent as a feather falling from the sky.

Eloise had decided, for an adventure, to take Me with her to borrow the Wizard's Grimoire, his book of spells. She had a pretty good idea that the Wizard wouldn't be very happy about it, which is why they were creeping around in the middle of the night.

"But isn't that like stealing," asked Me sagely.

"I'm not a thief, I'm a Princess," Eloise said rather primly.

"This is normal behaviour for a Princess is it?"

"When you get to know me better, you will find I'm not a normal Princess."

"Are you a naughty one then?"

That stopped Eloise in her tracks. Like everybody, Eloise liked to think well of herself, but was she, was she naughty?

"No, she replied, clearer and not haughtily like before. "I'm adventurous. I'm only borrowing the book, and when I've read it, I'll put it back."

"And, you know what you are doing?" asked Me worriedly, "We are not going to be turned into frogs?"

"No," replied Eloise, "that is princes who are turned into frogs, and you are definitely not a prince. Anyway," she brightened, "I have been having magic lessons with Zagoop the Wizard every day for as long as I can remember. It will be fine."

But now, tiptoeing down the passageway to the Wizard's spell chamber, Eloise wasn't so sure.

―――

"Have you used magic before," Me had asked before they left.

"My best magic was used against Zoltan, the Silver Dragon, to trick him, when I killed him with my dagger."

Although Me's face was not solid, and floated in front of her, there was a look in his eye that was a mixture of respect, and Eloise fancied, a little bit of fear. However, he just said a quiet "Oooh," and Eloise soon forgot about it.

―――

Eloise and Me were in the corridor outside the Wizard's chamber. Eloise as always was cool and confident, but was surprised to see how steady Me was.

"Ready?" she whispered into the dark.

Me just smiled and held up his thumb.

"Okay, can you pop through the wall and have a look inside please? See if there are any traps or dangers."

Me disappeared for a second, then materialised in front of Eloise looking a lot less cocky.

"What's the matter," asked the Princess, her tone confident.

"Maybe this isn't such a good idea."

"What's the matter?" asked Eloise impatiently.

"There's a monster."

"What does it look like?"

"A monster. I have never seen one before."

"How bad can it be? You had never seen a Princess and look how well that turned out."

"It's very big, with lots of sharp teeth, and worse than that, it talks."

"What did it say?"

"Good evening."

"Doesn't sound too bad." Eloise smiled. "Was it yellow with a lot of hair on its head?"

"Yes," said Me cautiously.

"That's okay," said Eloise, "that's Arnold. He is a Lion. He is very nice."

"Nice, for a talking monster?"

"He's not a monster, he is lovely, and of course he talks, he's friends with a Wizard."

Me was trying very hard to take all this in. "You mean he's not a pet, he's a friend of the Wizard?"

"Yes."

"And, you don't think he will tell the Wizard that you stole his book?"

"Oh no, Arnold is far too much of a gentleman, and anyway, we are borrowing it, not stealing it."

However, in the end, Eloise was mistaken.

Traditionally a young apprentice magician could only hold three spells at a time. Eloise, because she was a Princess, didn't think of herself as an apprentice magician, never mind a novice Wizard.

In the same way, she didn't think of herself as a Warrior, although like learning magic, she had been trained in the Warrior arts since she was a small child.

Unknown to Eloise, her mother, the Queen, had been a great Wizard, and Eloise had inherited her mother's gifts. Eloise wasn't just talented at magic, Eloise *was* magic.

When Eloise put her hand on the door handle, and slipped the key into the lock, the door refused to budge. There was a funny grating sound of laughter, and then the door itself spoke.

"This Wizard's door is shut quite tight
Although you try with all your might."

If Me had had skin, he would have jumped right out of it.

Straight away Eloise used one of the spells she had prepared. This of course was a door opening spell.

Because Zagoop the Wizard, the most powerful Wizard in the Kingdom, had locked his door with a mighty spell, normally an apprentice like Eloise wouldn't have the strength to countermand it. However, because Eloise was magic itself, her spell got stronger and stronger. In the end there was a loud bang, and the door vanished in a puff of smoke. From inside the Wizard's chamber came the mighty roar of a Lion.

"Eloise," cried Me desperately, "we'll wake up half the castle!"

"Don't be scared, Me."

"I'm not scared. This is the most exciting adventure I have ever had. That door exploding nearly blew my socks off."

"And mine," came a deep sonorous voice from within the chamber.

Eloise pushed on through the haze and fully into the chamber, to be confronted by a great lion with a huge and magnificent mane.

"Good evening, great and wise Arnold, friend of Zagoop the Wizard. I have come to borrow the Wizard's Grimoire."

"No child, you come like a thief in the night, and you shall not have the book. Go now, back to bed, and we shall hear no more about it."

Like all children, even princesses, Eloise didn't like being spoken to like a naughty child, which in a way she was. Even Me had suggested it. Hadn't she visited the mountain lair of the mighty Zoltan, The Silver Dragon, smooth talked him, and stabbed him through the heart?

Unfortunately, Eloise forgot her good graces and spoke to Arnold in a manner not befitting a princess. "No, old creature, move out of my way please."

"How, could you be so rude?" asked Me, as they continued deeper into the rooms of the Wizard's chamber.

"I did say please," said Eloise.

"Eloise," said Me in a distressed voice, "he is a great lion, the oldest friend of Zagoop the Wizard, and probably a friend of your father."

"Never mind that now," said Eloise, concentrating on the moment. "How long have we been walking down this corridor?"

"Oh about twenty minutes," replied Me, who didn't really walk, but glided everywhere.

"That's what I thought. We must be in a maze, or an enchanted corridor."

"Or both," said Me helpfully, "an enchanted maze."

Without realising it, Me was right. He and Eloise had unknowingly wandered into a magical maze.

"Have a look through the wall," suggested Eloise.

Obligingly, Me pushed his head through the wall to their left.

"What can you see?"

"I can see you!"

Eloise spun around, and there on the opposite wall of the passage was Me's head, protruding through.

"It really is a magical maze," sighed Eloise.

At that moment, the passage ended, and in front of Eloise and Me, was a large green wooden door with a heavy metal knocker shaped like a question mark. Eloise went straight up to the knocker, and banged it three times.

The door in front of them swung open, revealing a huge empty space. Without hesitation Eloise stepped into the void, with Me close behind her, and with a sound like thunder, the door slammed shut behind them.

There was a feeling of tremendous space, a giant cavern, just like in Zoltan's lair, but completely and utterly pitch black.

Eloise felt a tingle in her hand. Me must be holding it, but whether that was to comfort her, or reassure himself, she wasn't sure.

Suddenly, right in front of them, two giant malevolent eyes shone, as if someone had lit two lamps. Eloise's hand went to her sword, but it wasn't there. She had been off to borrow a book, not be confronted by monsters, and had left it hanging on her bedpost.

"Ah, but I'm not a monster," came a huge voice, "but you know who I am."

Eloise, all this time, had been cool, calm and collected. She stood small, but proud, as the nebulous light in the great cavern increased, revealing the gigantic head and coils of Zoltan, the Silver Dragon.

"You're not real," cried Eloise, "I have already finished with you."

"Are you so sure my child?" The dragon spoke softly, but the timbre of its voice made the stone floor shake. "Go back now, whilst you can."

"You're not real," reaffirmed Eloise. She was still stood, defiant, confident, and proud, and she was aware of Me standing with her, bravely by her side.

"I see you have brought a friend," said the dragon in a smarmy voice, "but he's not really here."

"He is more real, and wonderful than you will ever be," cried Eloise. "You are just a wizard's illusion to scare me away."

"So be it," said the dragon, and opened its huge tooth lined maw. Each giant tooth was bigger than Eloise. There was a glow of fire at the back of the dark cavernous throat, and a faint unpleasant whiff of sulphur and hot ashes.

Eloise could feel beads of moisture on her forehead forming from the heat. She turned to Me with a smile, and said, "Don't worry, it's all smoke and mirrors."

Me wasn't so sure, but he trusted Eloise, so he gave her the best smile he could muster, a difficult feat, when your face is wispy, like mist in the wind.

The fire at the back of the dragon's throat grew, and an exploding fireball flew out, and overwhelmed them with no thing.

Suddenly Eloise and Me were standing in the Wizard's study, before a large desk, where rested the Wizard's book of spells. Little lines of fire, lightning, and fizzes of energy ran across its cover.

Behind the desk stood the great lion, Arnold, the mighty wizard, Zagoop, and Eloise's father, the King.

The King was absolutely beside himself. It was later, and Eloise and her father were alone together in the Throne room. Eloise had never seen him so angry.

"I ..., I ..., I ...," he spluttered, "I've never been so humiliated in all my life. You broke into Zagoop's chamber, apparently to steal his Grimoire,"

"Borrow, not steal."

"Be quiet child," chided the King. "You broke in to Zagoop's chamber, and you were terribly rude to Arnold, his oldest and most respected friend."

"I only said, that I wanted to borrow the book."

"Be quiet child!"

Eloise quailed before her Father's wrath, and it was at this moment that Me chose to materialise.

"My goodness me," cried the King, "a ghost."

"This is my..." but Eloise trailed off, as Me held up his hand to silence her.

He stood bravely between Eloise and the King, and exuded a quiet dignity.

"Oh, wise and powerful King," he began. "Your daughter is

brave, and wise, and a credit to you. Since becoming my friend she has helped me to grow, to learn about the world, and to see my existence through wiser eyes, for her great gift to me has been Wisdom."

"And thievery and skulking," replied the King, not at all mollified.

"Eloise was training me to be brave and face my fears, so borrowing the book uninvited was a part of that training."

The King looked at the ghost shielding his daughter, and the defiant young lady behind him, and softening, sat down on his throne.

"Tell me Eloise, is this the boy you spoke to me about, and asked my help?"

"Yes Father."

"Then I'm sorry my child for not taking you seriously. I see you have done an excellent job without my help. What is your name young man?" he said, turning back to the ghost.

"Me, Sire."

"Really, how unusual. I'm pleased to meet you," he said graciously to the ghost. "As you seem to have acquired so much wisdom and courage, and been a true and brave friend to my daughter, I hereby appoint you Royal Advisor to the Princess Eloise."

Me hovered by the throne, proudly beaming.

"Eloise I'm afraid that despite your good works, I must still punish you for being so rude to Arnold. For a month, every day before breakfast, and after supper, you must brush down Rupert and all the other horses in the stable."

"Oh, thank you Father," she cried jumping up to hug him tight, for after all that was no punishment at all.

FORTY TWO

"HOW MANY KLINGONS does it take to change a light bulb?"

"How long's a piece of string?" someone shouted.

"Is not the right answer."

"Forty two," yelled someone else.

"Not, Life, the Universe, and everything. We're talking Roddenberry, not Adams."

"Have you got the faintest idea what they are talking about?" asked the squirrel of the Mockingbird.

"Star Trek," the bird tweeted.

"Excuse me Madame," a waiter addressed the mocking bird, "the management don't encourage either sardonic attitudes, or the use of mobile phones."

"No," whispered the storyteller, "it wasn't that kind of tweet."

"Are you having a laugh?" interjected the squirrel, feeling the need to maintain a place in the conversation.

"Well he hasn't finished the joke yet."

The slowly evolving life form that had only recently been spawned in a petri dish decided to narrow its options. Unfortunately as it only appeared as a dirty smear on the glass surface, it was unlikely that anyone was going to take it seriously.

Interrupted by a small burst of applause, the smear had a moment of honest reflection before being flushed down the sink by an over zealous lab technician.

BILLY WHIZZ

A LOT of people think that Billy Whizz was just a character in the Beano comic, drawn by the Thompson family in Scotland. They were graphic artists.

There has been a recent discovery of identical cave art from stone age times in both India and Brazil. Of course the archeologists, who think that the Giza pyramids were built with earth ramps, were completely baffled.

There were far thinking Quantum scientists and spiritual mystics who thought the artists may have shared a universal consciousness. If anyone had bothered to ask Mr Thomson of Glascow, Scotland, he would have told them that the single artist responsible for both paintings and forty six yet to be discovered, was in fact the original Billy Whizz.

At this moment in time Billy is the earliest known graffiti artist in history, although I'm sure that posterity will find more.

Billy was from a time one hundred and forty thousand years ago, give or take, many millennia before the existence of Buddha. He belonged to an obscure sect of spiritual mystics, so advanced that they had developed psychic powers of cell regeneration, psychokinesis, telepathy, and most importantly the ability to travel through space by telekinesis.

Belonging to a spiritual sect that encouraged the expression of creativity, Billy Whizz was a very talented artist and musician. Being naturally modest, the Bingawingers, for that was their name, lived in beautiful crystal towers that glittered in the light of the sun, and required no decoration, for nothing could compete with this natural beauty.

Art then, was a private affair performed simply for the joy of creative expression, so important for developing and maintaining their spirituality. Billy would seek out special caves, deep underground, and paint his beautiful pictures. Just like the present day street artists of New York painting their work on the sides of buildings and trains, they all had their signature marks. Billy's was based on the musical notation of his favourite song that he had written and sung. A repeating choral harmony in thirteen parts. You may think that for all that his art was unique, hidden deep below ground, only for his own artist expression, and unshared with the world, the fact that he signed his work in this way, showed a degree of ego unexpected in a great spiritual master.

Anyway such was the question Mr Thompson asked Billy on their first meeting in 1934 when Billy visited him, having finally mastered travel through the space time continuum.

Why Billy Whizz visited Mr Thompson in this way, leading him to develop the Billy Whizz character in his famous comic, is actually a deeper mystery than the two pictures found at opposite sides of the Earth.

Now Mr Thomspon is dead, I guess his grandson, Algernon William Whizz Thompson, myself, at your service, is the only one capable of spilling the beans, and actually, I won't be doing so. After all a secret is a secret.

JANE

JANE SAT down in the airport lounge pretending to read a newspaper she had picked up on the plane. Who remembered now the days of newspapers waiting as you boarded your flights? Of course that was the old days of economy flights, before all the cheapo companies like Easy Jet came along, and Jane had flown first class. Hard to imagine now, but back in those days people were allowed to smoke on flights. Some changes were for the better she thought as she pretended to read her paper.

Jane had to pretend because this paper was printed in kanji and she neither read or spoke Chinese. Chinese, again the assumptions of the ignorant west. If you were studying Chinese at University you would study at least two different languages, Mandarin, the ancient language of the bureaucratic class, and probably Cantonese, the language of Hong Kong. Jane spoke several European languages fluently, but didn't speak Chinese.

"You want read paper?" a voice next to her spoke in broken Parisian French. Jane turned to look at a wizened old woman who was both clearly oriental and very very old. She was dressed in a shapeless smock of some grey colour that Jane was sure had never made it to the catwalks, had ancient straw sandals on dirty feet with horrible uncut toenails and a hat that Jane decided was made from some type of antique cardboard rammed down tight on her head, and held in place by string tied in a neat bow under a wrinkled and bristly chin. She was offering today's edition of Paris Match.

"No thank you, Madame," Jane replied in a similar Parisian accent, "I already have one."

"The Shanghai Times," the old woman snorted. "I can tell you can't read it."

"And who are you?" Jane asked. "The Chinese Mata Hari?"

"No my dear, I am your friend," and with that she clapped her hands and there was a blinding flash of light. When Jane's vision returned to normal she found she was sat on an embroidered cushion on the floor of a beautifully decorated room with silk hangings and beautiful ink paintings of birds of paradise and calligraphy. Opposite her the old lady sat comfortably on a cushion, now dressed in a flowing kimono, her sleek white hair formally arranged into a neat bun with two carved ebony sticks arranged at angles that Jane instinctively knew were both ancient and perfect.

Between them on the floor was a small charcoal stove, a gleam of red coals with a wisp of smoke from sandalwood incense, a beautiful, old, round iron kettle gently steaming. Next to the stove was an exquisite little tea set of two tiny porcelain bowls and a tea pot, beautifully painted with a golden dragon.

"Jasmine," the old lady said, this time in English, with a home counties accent, and a slight bow of the head.

"Yes please," Jane replied calmly, as if surreal and polite abductions were a normal part of her day, "and do you have any jammy dodgers?"

AUNT GERTRUDE

AUNT GERTRUDE WOKE up and felt damp and uncomfortable. Somebody had considerately laid yesterday's Financial Times over her, to presumably keep her warm, and it was both pink and damp. Her back felt draughty and wretched from the hard wooden slats on the bench that had become her bed.

"Roast potatoes?," said a kindly voice.

"Fried celeriac," responded Aunt Gertrude.

"No, no," repeated the kindly voice, "would you like some roast potatoes?"

"For breakfast?"

"I'm afraid my dear lady," came the voice, "that it is now past twelve midday, and we are heading into luncheon time."

"Luncheon time," cried Aunt Gertrude. "In Hastings!"

"I'm afraid you aren't in Hastings Madam."

"Not in Hastings."

"No Madam. I'm afraid you are in Rotherham."

"The slippy cat wheedled the rubbery fish."

"Tongue twister?"

"Certainly not."

"You seem to be in some distress. Can I please be of assistance?"

"You and your roast potatoes?"

"Yes Madam."

"Have you got any horseradish?"

"Roast potatoes would be a sorry affair without it Madam."

"And gravy?"

"Gravy Madam. I think Madam is mistaking me for the Maitre D' at the Savoy Grill."

"Oh no, you're not a bit like sweet Gerald."

"Perhaps you would like me to call him."

"Would you be so kind. I'm sure he will have some gravy."

Aunt Gertrude was tiring of this absurd conversation. Taking a slightly damp handkerchief from her blouse pocket, she brought it to her lipstick smeared mouth, spat on it, and used it to wipe the crusted sleep from her eyes. Her ablutions complete, she returned her begrimed hankie to her pocket, and grasping the edge of the bench with surprisingly strong hands, pulled herself into a sitting position, and opened her eyes to face the day.

THE TASTE OF HEAVEN

THE HUBBLE BUBBLE Tea Company Chief Executive, or Cha Wobble, as he was known, rang the gong on another day. It was an exciting time. They had developed a new old tea. New to Andromeda, ancient for the Earth.

The Earth, that near neighbour of primitive barbarity, and yet.

It was in many ways the tea that had called out to him. He had tasted it in a dream. Unlike anything that was grown on the fertile terraces of Andromeda's planets.

In his dream he had been knelt on a wooden veranda of a beautiful but simple building surrounded by beautiful plants of thick tubular stems that seemed to have grown in sections. On the ground to his left, polished flat rocks of great beauty had been set into a mossy carpet, creating a footpath of stepping stones.

In front of Wobble was a young human in a black jacket and baggy trousers, also kneeling. Before him he had a small beautiful ceramic bowl of great aesthetic wonder that kindled something in Wobble's two hearts. Slightly offset between them there was a form of primitive stove in a thick metal bowl, with black carbon glowing with fire, that was heating an old iron pot. The human with simple deft movements lifted the lid, placing it on a small section of the same plant from the garden, but old and dry, and then used a ladle made from the same simple organic matter to pour boiling water from the pot into the bowl. He then picked up another piece of organic tube whose end had been carved into a hundred delicately curved tines and proceeded to whisk the water, occasionally removing his whisk to inspect it. Satisfied, he placed it back on the floor mat with great reverence.

Wobble knelt entranced, not aware of any discomfort in his folded legs.

After removing a small black plastic looking container from a silken bag that was itself a work of art, the human took a fine silken cloth from his robe and carefully and ceremoniously wiped it with defined deft movements. Appearing satisfied, although no expression changed on his face which remained calmly serene, he took a flat wooden stick that reminded Wobble of a spatula, and spooned a fine green powder into the bowl. He then ladled more boiling water from the pot to the bowl and began to whisk the mixture with one hand, whilst holding the bowl steady with the other. Even these movements were defined, rhythmic, and ceremonial.

Wobble's undisciplined mind wondered how much different it would be if he was attempting this ceremony with his four arms. Looking down at the two palms resting on his thighs he realised that he must be in the body of a human.

When the human seemed content with his activity he carefully with great care and love laid down his whisk. Holding the bowl he held it firmly in his two hands, rotating it by degrees, until satisfied he placed it on the floor before Wobble and for the first time spoke one simple world which Wobble understood was, "Please."

Taking the proffered bowl, Wobble feeling what was required of him, firmly lifted it with his two hands. Looking with love at the frothy green mixture in the simple dish he rotated the bowl in a similar way to the human, instinctively knowing what was right, and raising the rim of the bowl to his lips he loudly slurped on the taste of heaven.

PHILISTINES

RAIN KEEPS FALLING.

Everyone was blaming the global warming for the weather. Man's toxic influence on the planet. According to their own scientists each year Earth's volcanos belch out more carbon dioxide than all man had created since the start of the industrial revolution. Go figure.

The kids thought it was chem trails. Some conspiracy about bad people seeding the skies to create storms.

Bixa Boxjob knew the truth about the weather on Earth. I guess, he thought, that it was a conspiracy, although to his knowledge no one had offered an accurate theory about it.

After all, it all was all down to that old chestnut, revenge. You see Bixa was an artist. When the crop circles started appearing there was plenty of speculation on Earth about flying saucers. For Earth that was pretty wild speculation, not really a conspiracy. It was more of a conspiracy, or just lack of imagination, to try and work out how they could be created by humans.

Some artists draw on paper. Some artists draw on canvas. These days some artists draw on computers. Bixa had grander canvases to display his talents. Bixa liked to draw on planets.

FORTY TWO

Crop circles were just doodles really. Just quick sketches done over night. Just as on Earth where artists will dash off the odd charcoal sketch or water colour to pay the rent, whereas their real passion is in their oils. Bixa's real passion lay in his desert work. He had used up the only available space in Peru, South America long ago. Giant pictures of humming birds and spiders that can only be seen from space or in flight. That was Bixa's medium. Bixa was immensely proud of his work. Having exhausted the Earth he had moved on to other planets but like on Earth the constancy of the media was a problem. Bixa had done some of his best work on the Saharan desert. It was great for practice, but barely lasted one of the Earth days.

Some of the work Bixa was most pleased with was on the far side of the moon. The landscape was just perfect. Large deserts. No weather.

Being proud of his work Bixa was delighted when mankind discovered his pictures in the Nazca desert. Instead of admiring his art they just speculated on how primitive man could have created it. He had got really excited when man finally left the planet and got into space, even if it was only as far as its orbiting moon. Finally man was going to see some of his best work.

But nothing. How can you keep something like that under wraps. Well, man's normal way of course. Misinformation, secrecy, assassination. Something worthy of conspiracy.

Bixa was so disappointed. Just because you belong to a hyper intelligent advanced race of beings capable of planet art doesn't mean you won't be irascible when your ego is rattled.

Bixa in a moment of pique decided to wipe his art from the Earth. He created a change in the flow of the oceans that in time would create more and more severe storms that would wipe his beautiful creations away. If the primitive ingrates who inhabited Earth were wiped away too, then he wasn't going to shed any tears for a little collateral damage.

ELOISE AND THE WATER SERPENT

THE LITTLE BLUE butterfly flapped its wings hovering over the fragrant flowers. The princess watched the bejewelled light twinkling off its silken wings and marvelled in the moment.

With a flash of sudden movement a green tongue shot out into the void and wrapped around the gossamer sails beating in the summer rays, crushing them with its ferocity. The princess just had time to see the last feeble twitches as the remains of the beautiful insect were dragged into the gaping slimy maw of the smiling toad.

The princess smiled at the toad for wasn't it beautiful too. She admired the way its warty skin seemed to absorb the light. Its bright bulbous eyes seemed to hold her, and the meadow was full of their smiles.

"Eloise," came a cry from far away, and gathering up her skirts, the young girl reached out with lightning speed, grasped the surprised amphibian with both hands, planting a big kiss on its slimy mouth. Then, carefully and gently she placed it back on its rock, and with a wave she was off racing towards the castle, her golden curls trailing in the summer breeze.

Eloise was sitting in a rocking chair by the hearth enjoying the warmth of the roaring fire, and shelling peas for Bella, the King's head cook. She took a pod from the box by her seat, enjoying the feeling as she popped it with her fingers, then running her thumb nail along the green inner flesh, releasing the little green spheres to drop into the colander in her lap.

A sudden chill brushed her, and without looking up from her task, she warmly greeted her special friend. "Hello Me," she said brightly.

"Talking to yourself again," asked the cook, who had overheard. "You need to get out more my girl, and find some friends."

"I'm talking to my friend," Eloise replied.

"I mean proper friends, little girls like you that you can play with, not imaginary friends."

But Me wasn't an imaginary friend at all. He was the ghost of a little boy who had died long ago in the King's castle, and he was Eloise's very bestest friend.

———

He could taste breakfast.

It was a calm beautiful morning and the surface of the lake was mirror calm. Calm that is except for the giant ripple he created as a swam towards his meal.

Eloise sometimes liked to come out on to the lake. There was an old rowboat in the castle boathouse that she liked to take out early in the morning. She enjoyed the calm serenity of the lake, and the ache in her arms and shoulders as she pulled the oars of the small craft, skimming over the silent waters.

She had a particular favourite spot, out of sight of the castle walls, where she liked to ship the oars, and just float gazing out at the reflective surface of the water, watching the light, the patterns it made, and how it was affected by the silken wings of the occasional dragon or damsel fly.

He could almost taste his breakfast now. Like a shark is said to be able to detect a drop of blood in the ocean a mile away so too, could the monster of the lake, sense the beating heart up ahead.

Still he reflected, it was a beautiful heart. Strong and brave, and sure he suspected, joined to a clever and inquisitive mind. Ooh, he trembled, my favourite.

Eloise was sitting in the bottom of the boat, on an old woollen blanket, with her arms resting on the side next to the rowlock, looking out over the aquamarine surface. Up ahead she could see a small bump in the water. Was it a small log, or something floating. It seemed to be getting bigger. Perhaps it was a little wave caused by the jumping of one of the lake's giant carp.

He was still quite a long way away when Eloise spotted him, but he felt a frisson of excitement, knowing his breakfast had made a connection.

Yes, it was like a wave, Eloise decided. It was like a giant ripple and seemed to be heading straight towards her. At this moment, not sensing any danger, Eloise was intrigued by this new development in her morning boating excursion.

He could feel her now. Yes, wise, intelligent, brave. He suspected she was thoroughly charming. He would swallow her whole, not spoil her biting or chewing, but feel her wriggling as he swallowed her down. Perfect. He smiled at the thought, and as his great jaws stretched sideways, the size of the ripple increased.

Eloise was standing now, perfectly at balance, in the gentle rocking boat. She saw a gentle ripple from her movement spread out into the waiting surface at the same time as the approaching wave suddenly doubled in size. Feeling calm, and excited, she was aware of an increased beating in her chest and a sudden dryness in her mouth.

Ah, the change in her heart. He could tell now, it was a girl. So strong, such power. Its stronger beat called out to him, urging him on, and with a whip of his mighty tail, he accelerated towards his delicate morsel.

Eloise was calmness itself. She didn't know what was making the wave, but she could see that it was heading straight for her. It was coming too fast to avoid or row away from. No one was a witness to her plight. No one was coming to her aid, not even Me. Without taking her eyes off the approaching danger, she reached down into the boat and lifting up one of the oars. She held if firmly in both hands, like a giant sword, with its flattened end pointing outwards towards the growing wave.

Oh joy, cried the monster to himself. The little girl is going to fight me.

The wave was growing rapidly now. Only a hundred feet away it was as big as a cart. Suddenly the surface of the water broke apart revealed huge gaping jaws, its black skin shining through the rain of droplets, glittering in the early morning sun, punctuated by great pointed glistening white teeth. Eloise held firm, her bare feet gripping the smooth wooden planks and the oaken oar comfortable in her grasp. As the great maw grew closer and closer, she caught a sight of large luminescent eyes set in a huge serpents head. They were kind and smiling and concentrated on her, and Eloise knew she was in serious trouble.

As he lifted his head a little, the curtain of water broke apart, and he saw the girl for the first time. How magnificent she looked, standing there in her little boat, eyes locked on him, as she proudly held her weapon before her. Long curls of golden hair hung around a beautiful young face. But her eyes, so pretty and blue, yet the eyes of a warrior, the eyes of a princess. My caviar he thought happily, and with a sudden beat of his tail he launched up out of the water before powering down into its depths.

Eloise gasped as a great head reared out of the water in front of her, before crashing down disappearing below the lake's surface, now raging with the tsunami created by its mighty splash.

The great wave raced towards her, breaking up the mirrored calm and causing the floor of her boat to rock. Just as the huge wave was about to overwhelm her with a deafening roar of water, and the monster's triumph, she shot up into the air. As she span in a rainbow of water droplets and sunshine, a part of her mind relished the beauty of the moment. She felt her feet lose contact with the wood as the splintered boat broke apart around her. Still gripping the oar in her strong young hands she felt gravity reclaiming her, and looking down she saw the waiting jaws of the black monster widely agape, and began her journey downwards.

As Eloise fell towards the monster's spread jaws her mind flashed to the great clock in the Castle stateroom. The Jane clock. This magic clock, instead of the normal two hands for the hours and minutes, had multiple hands that told the time simultaneously in many realms. When the hands coincided the clock disappeared, only to reappear later. No one knew where or why it went. Eloise suddenly realised the solution to her problem was to align the monster to half past twelve.

All these thoughts took place within a fraction of a second. Pivoting her body in mid air like an acrobat, she saw the monsters jaws below her and rotated the oar horizontally in her downward racing arms to slot into line and dropped like a diver into the gap. Passing the teeth she fell into the darkness of its great mouth until the edges of the oar ground into the gristle of the monsters palate bringing Eloise to a sudden halt. The unexpected de-acceleration almost broke her tight grip on the oar and her legs and feet dragged along the beasts sandpaper like tongue, breaking her fall, whilst making her want to scream from the skin being chaffed from her legs.

"Oh, you clever wicked girl," Eloise heard in her mind, "I hope you can swim," and with that the monster started sinking back into the lake. Like a bath emptying down a giant plug hole, the water began to pour over its teeth and fill the monsters throat like water pouring into a well. The pull of gravity on Eloise's arms, was massively increased by the tons of water falling on her head and shoulders, Just before she was plunged into total darkness she took a mighty gulp of air and clamped her mouth tight shut as she was totally submerged in water still clinging to the oar embedded in the great serpents mouth as it dropped down into the depths, all the time its mocking laughter ringing in her ears. Letting go of the oar, Eloise kicked her legs as powerfully as she could, surging upwards out of the beasts mouth, the air in her lungs helping to lift her up. Her eyes watched the great teeth pass by as she raced to the light above. She burst through from one realm into another, her lungs screaming for air, as she gasped into the beautiful world and sucked in its life giving oxygen. A good and confident swimmer, she was exhausted, and weakly kicked her legs to tread water, weighed down by her sodden dress and still gasping for air.

Just when she thought things couldn't get any worse, her kicking feet scraped on smooth skin and suddenly she was out of the water lying face down on the head of the mighty monster.

"Lie still child," the voice whispered in her mind. She was in shock, and unusually for her, Eloise obeyed. She could see that they were heading towards the shore, and with surprising agility she pushed up and sat cross legged on the great head as it plowed over the surface of the lake, heading towards the glitter of a sandy beach.

The boy awoke. He was wet and cold and realised with a shudder that he had no clothes on. The ground was cold and damp below him. A hazy memory tugged at his mind. A beautiful smile, a beautiful face, and yes, a beautiful kiss.

Eloise was thinking fast. What did the monster want with her? what happened when they arrived at the shore of the lake.

"I'm not going to eat you child," came into her mind. "I have already tried that, and look where that got me."

"Then what do you want," replied Eloise, talking with just her mind as if it were the most natural thing in the world.

"Oh, dear child, a friend at the very least. Maybe a student."

"I already have a tutor, said Eloise haughtily, "what would you teach me?"

"Oh, special things."

"Like what?" asked Eloise thoroughly intrigued, and seemingly not terribly mindful that she had only just escaped being breakfast,

"How to ride a moon beam," threw in the mighty serpent.

"Easy," replied Eloise. "In my imagination."

"Yes, my child. You see you have so much potential. I can teach you how to access it and release it."

"What moon beams?"

"No child, your potential."

"And stop calling me your child." said Eloise. My mummy is dead and she was a queen. My daddy is King of all this land."

"Oh little princess, what fun we are going to have together. And stop calling me a monster, it's very rude."

"What should I call you?"

"Charles."

"Charles?"

"Yes, Charles."

"Why?" asked Eloise.

"Simple." replied Charles, "It's my name."

"Well, Charles," said Eloise, who was thoroughly enjoying both their conversation, and riding on Charles' head as they sped over the lakes surface towards the looming shore. "What's next?"

"Well, for one thing," answered Charles in her mind, " you can get this wretched stick out of my throat, it's exceedingly uncomfortable."

"You should have thought of that," said Eloise, "before you ate me." And with the poise of both a warrior and a princess she elegantly leapt from Charles' head on to the shingle beach and turned to look in to the giant benevolent eyes of her new friend and teacher.

"You've made friends with what?" asked Me incredulously.

"A giant serpent I met in the lake. His name is Charles, and he was going to eat me," said Eloise in a rush, "but I escaped, and now he's my friend, and he's going to teach me how to release my potential."

"Your potential?"

"Yes my potential."

"Eloise, princess of the realm, warrior girl who tricked and killed the Silver Dragon saving the realm. Eloise who mastered magic. Eloise who alone in all the kingdom can talk to ghosts?"

"One ghost."

"Yes, one ghost," replied Me testily. "One ghost who is finding it hard to grasp how this giant water snake who tried to eat his best friend, can know the first thing about her potential, never mind help it to grow."

"You had to be there," said Eloise and ignoring the enraged shade, carried on eating her porridge that Abby had given her for breakfast.

The key grated in the door. The Boy was silent, barely daring to breathe. He thought the whole castle would wake up and fall crashing about his ears.

The princess stirred in her sleep, feeling the echo, not from the mechanical noise from the grating of the key, but the increased beating of a heart, that was opening a door in hers.

The boy could feel his heart beating in his chest, like a great clanging bell in his mind, and yet the early morning darkness at the castle door was as silent as before.

"Can I help you please?" a confident voice spoke in the darkness, right by his ear. The boy would have jumped, but he had been endowed with a good and true heart, and although very surprised, and to be honest, a little frightened, he seemed to have control of his beating heart, so that when he replied his voice likewise was calm and steady.

"Yes please," he replied, "I wonder if this is the right way to visit the Princess."

"The right way," echoed the voice, "the right way to visit the princess. And which princess would that be laddie, that you come creeping about the castle gates in the middle of the night?"

"I'm afraid I don't know her name," said the Boy.

"Don't know her name. Don't know her name," repeated the owner of the voice, who was beginning to thoroughly enjoy himself. "Don't know the name of her royal highness, our beautiful princess, and yet, here you come sneaking at the castle door."

"I'd know her again if I was introduced to her," continued the boy bravely, ignoring the implied slur on his integrity.

"Would you now, my laddie, would you now. And how would you be doing that?"

"By the touch of her lips."

"By the touch of her lips," replied the voice, now beginning to seethe with indignation.

"Yes, by the touch of her lips, from when she awoke me with a kiss."

"With a kiss?" the voice almost shouted.

"Now listen," said the boy, seeds of righteousness growing in his heart, "I don't like your attitude. "What is your name?" And reaching into his pocket he brought out a box of matches, took a wooden match from inside, feeling the bumpy end with his finger, and with a note of defiance, loudly struck it along the side of the box. The sudden light filled the space illuminating the gnarled wood of the old castle door with its polished brass lock and handle, but of his interrogator there was no sign. He was completely alone.

"Mmmmmmmmmmm!"

"What are you doing?"

Me span around, surprised and caught off guard. He was in front of one of the huge gold framed mirrors in a deserted corridor of the east wing of the castle. His face was all screwed up in concentration and he was making the Mmm sound between gritted teeth.

"Nothing."

"Really, Me," repeated Eloise to the ghost, "what are you doing?"

"Don't want to say."

"Don't be ridiculous. Please, Me, please tell me what is going on?"

"I'm trying to see myself in the mirror."

"Oh, Me," laughed Princess Eloise, "whatever for."

"I knew you'd laugh," said Me in a hurt tone of voice.

"But Me, you are a ghost."

"You can see me."

"Yes Me, and you are very handsome."

"I don't want to be handsome."

"Then what do you want?"

"Nothing," replied Me, and after that he disappeared, and Eloise wondered what was going on with her friend.

"You found him doing what," asked her father, the King.

"He was floating in front of one of the large mirrors in the East wing, with a look of terrible concentration on his face, murmuring to himself.

"Ah," said the King. "And did he tell you what he was doing?"

"Not really, or not the whole truth anyway," divined Eloise. "He said he was trying to see himself in the mirror."

"Ah," said the King.

"Do you know what is going on Father?"

"Yes, I think I do."

"Please tell me Father."

"Let me ask you a question. Who can see Me, besides you?"

"No one that I know of," replied Eloise.

"Ah," said the King.

"Oh, Father, do tell me."

"I think he wants to be seen, by someone else besides you."

"But why would he want that?"

"Perhaps you should ask him."

"Thank you Father," replied Eloise, jumping up and kissing the King on his cheek, before running off out of the royal bedroom. How lucky she was to have a father who was a king that didn't encourage all that bowing and scraping. She had heard of kingdoms where everyone had to bow or curtesy to the monarch, even princes and princesses to their own parents. How lucky she was to have a lovely father who she could go to with her problems, especially as her mother had died when she was young. Still, Eloise could be a secretive girl. She had originally kept her ghost friend, Me, a secret, and although she had told Me about her new friend from the lake, she hadn't told her Father. As she skipped happily back towards the kitchens it never occurred to her that they could be connected.

―――

"But you eat people?"

"Oh, I'm very lucky to actually get humans, but yes if I can. I especially like eating children."

"Children?" said Eloise, shocked.

"Oh, yes," he continued. "So sweet, and juicy, delicious."

"Oh, you are so very very wicked," said Eloise.

"Yes, I am child, yes I am."

Eloise was sat in the sand on the edge of the lake, looking into the great glistening eyes of the giant serpent, whose huge scaled head protruded out of the water. It was strange at first, but now she hardly wondered about how all their conversations took place in her head. She knew that the monster was so huge and quick that he could snap her up in a single bite should he so desire, yet she felt quite safe in this close proximity to his huge mouth full of razor sharp teeth. He was her friend, and her trust was based on that friendship, and an understanding that Charles truly valued her. She had started as breakfast, but had become something more than a delicious meal. Yet, what was Charles to her she asked herself? A mentor? Another teacher? A friend? How could she be a friend with a monster who delighted in eating children?

She thought of one of her favourite books in the castle library, Everyone was scared of the ticking crocodile who had nearly made a meal of the wicked old pirate, but nobody became friends with him. Not even the pirate.

Eloise who had been given a thorough grounding in right and wrong was quite conflicted with her new friend, and Me had been very unhappy when she told him about Charles. In fact he had been very sulky of late, especially since their meeting in the East wing.

"What do you eat when you can't get children?"

"Fish mostly. The waters are full of large carp. Seals, dolphins, even turtles if I can get them."

"Stop, stop," cried Eloise. "Have you no shame?"

"No my child," replied Charles. "What did you have for dinner last night?"

"A salmon mousse, quail pâté with gooseberry jam, roast lamb with rosemary and garlic, and strawberries in aspic."

"And you call me wicked, child?"

"There is no comparison," said Eloise in her confident voice.

"It's more wicked to eat a turtle than a baby sheep?"

Eloise thought about what Charles had said, and as she did a large tear broke loose from her eye and trickled down her cheek. She noticed a change in the serpents eyes, which seemed to regard her with compassion.

Eloise was at a complete loss. Wiping away the tear with her sleeve, not the right behaviour for a princess a part of her whispered, she pushed herself up from the sand, and turning her back on the monster, wandered slowly on the path back to the castle.

"Goodbye child," came quietly in her mind, then just the wind whistling in the dunes, and the sting of tears in her eyes.

———

Eloise was lying in her four poster feather bed in her room in the palace. It was dark outside, and the room was full of the beautiful warbling music of bird song. She could feel it in her bones, it was going to be a wonderful day.

"Oh how right you are child," a strong voice spoke in her mind, "how right you are."

Eloise was excited. She jumped out of bed, and unerringly made her way to her closet. This was a room within a room. Rack after rack of beautiful gowns and dresses which rarely saw the light of day. She comfortably slipped into the dark room, knowing her way around through her young lifetime's familiarity. She was just pulling on an old pair of dirty jodhpurs which lay discarded on the back of a chair, when she jumped at a new voice in her ear.

"And where are you going in the middle of the night without a bye or a leave?"

"For goodness sake Me," Eloise said to the ghost, "you must

stop sneaking up on me like that. And what on earth are you doing in my closet? What's wrong with you?"

"I wasn't watching," said Me hurriedly. "I just followed you in. I'm worried about you."

"Worried about me? I'd be worried about you, Me, if my father, the King finds out you've been sneaking around my bed chamber."

"What's he going to do?" Me asked confidently, "cut my head off?"

"Good point," laughed Eloise,"there's not a lot he can do to a ghost. "Still," she asked her friend, "what are you doing in my bedroom so early in the morning?"

"You are going to sneak off out of the palace to meet with him, aren't you?"

"Yes," replied Eloise, "are you jealous? Oh, my goodness," sighed Eloise in surprised understanding, "you are."

"I am not jealous," Me replied in a hurt voice, "I'm worried about you. How can you trust this monster who you admitted did his very best to eat you up for breakfast. What's to stop him gobbling you up?"

"You had to be there," replied Eloise, "I know he seems very bad and wicked, and he eats children and beautiful creatures like dolphins and octopi, but he's old and wise, and he respects me."

"And that makes him your friend who you trust with your life?"

"Yes," replied the princess.

"I give up."

And from the sudden feeling of silence and emptiness in the room, Eloise knew that Me had gone.

―――――

"Where's your friend?"

"Good morning to you too," said Eloise.

The giant serpent arched a huge brow over a huge eye, and Eloise knew he was waiting for an answer.

"If you mean Me, he disappeared."

"In a huff?"

"I think so."

"Are you worried about him?"

"A little bit. He seemed rather upset, and he's very worried about my friendship with you."

"Thinks I'm going to eat you?"

"Yes," replied Eloise.

"Well we can't sit here sulking on the beach all day. Things to do, places to see, conversations to have."

"Really?"

"Yes really. Come on, jump aboard. The day is still young."

"Okay," said Eloise, and with a spring, jumped easily onto Charle's head and made herself comfortable for the journey to come.

———

"Woooooooooooooo," screamed Eloise at the top of her voice. "Wooooooooooooo!"

"Are you having fun child?"

"Oh yes," replied the Princess, "such fun."

The great lake, that had seemed endless was not. After several hours sitting cross legged on Charle's head, she found they were approaching huge cliffs. His scaly skin was soft and leathery, like chamois, and the scales created a texture, that with the smooth but rapid movement across the water was certainly as comfortable as sitting on the saddle of Rupert, her beautiful horse.

Though the ride and beautiful scenery were stimulating, the journey across the lake had held the most amazing conversation. Well, not so much as a dialogue, more of a monologue, as Charles did most of the talking, but with the occasional interjection and question from Eloise, which Charles encouraged, seemingly to have endless patience with her bright and enquiring mind.

"And did Celzius, the great Wizard, recover when the invisibility spell went wrong, and his skin became transparent, so that all his bones, organs, and giblets became visible?"

"Oh yes," my child, "but only after many months of suffering, and only then with the help of the Magus Malfeceint."

"The one who lived in a castle in the clouds?"

"Yes my child, literally, rather than figuratively."

"What big words you use Grandma," she joked, echoing one of her favourite stories.

"All the better to educate you," replied Charles joining in the fun.

"And did he reverse the spell by invoking ether energy magic," she enquired.

"I'm glad you have been paying attention, my child. Yes, he was able to reverse the symbiont field before the change became permanent."

"And why did he suffer so greatly," asked Eloise, "was he in pain?"

"Not physical my child. The failed spell only made his skin invisible, revealing the inside of his body for all the world to see. He tried to cover himself with cloaks. Even the thickest pelt from an Ailephant would be affected by the spell and be as clear as his invisible skin."

"Like the Emperor's new clothes, but actually real," laughed Eloise.

"Precisely child," agreed Charles, pleased at her comprehension.

"So it was the horror, pity, and revulsion that was mirrored in the eyes of all he met on his journey's that caused him so much pain."

Eloise felt the subtle nod of Charle's head, distinguishing it from the sometimes bumpy ride as they raced across the still water of the lake, leaving a strong wake in their passing that split the lake in a most pleasing fashion, if you happened to be an observant and aesthetic bird or dragon flying overhead.

Up ahead Eloise saw a rapidly approaching break in the cliffs, and what she could now detect as a mighty roaring sound that seemed to fill her ears with its power.

As they raced towards the gap, the roaring got louder and louder, and the air was full of spray and mist. Eloise could feel the rush of wind blowing her hair behind her, and the sting of water in her eyes. Up ahead there just seemed to be empty space rippling with rainbows forming in the moist air, then suddenly they were plunging into the void, out and down over the lip of a mighty waterfall. Eloise who thought she might burst from excitement, had never felt more alive.

"Woooooooooooooooooooo," she cried.

It was like they had fallen off the edge of the world.

Like those simple people in ancient times who believed that the earth was flat and if you sailed to the edge you would fall off into who knows what. It was a terrifying plunge into nothing. The cascading roar of water paralleled their descent, and Eloise's joy and excitement had changed to terror.

"Charles," she screamed, "we are going to die."

"Why of course not, my child, you are going to save us."

"How?" yelled Eloise, with her mind, for all their conversation was telepathic.

"With your magic my dear."

All this time they were dropping into the darkening abyss, the wind tearing at Eloise's eyes, compressing the skin on her face.

"I do not know a spell to save us."

"I said with your magic child."

"Charles, I don't have any magic."

"Eloise, princess of this land, you are magic."

And with an explosion of love and serenity in her heart, she knew it was true, and with a curving swoop the mighty serpent came out of his downward plunge and defying gravity flew back to the light.

———

"Why didn't I fall off?"

They were flying in level flight high high above the lake now. Eloise felt she could see the whole world but knew it was but a tiny part.

"With the changing acceleration? The vertical flight back up?"

"Yes. How is it possible?"

"My child you powered my flight, are powering my flight. I am a serpent of the seas and lakes. Do you see any wings? If you can do such a thing, surely you can keep your seat when things become a little turbulent."

"Turbulent," laughed Eloise, "I've never been so scared in my life."

"Yet here we are," said Charles in a complacent tone, "here we are."

"And it's so very beautiful," said Eloise. "Thank you Charles."

"Your welcome my child, you are truly welcome."

———

Eloise ran up the beach and through the dunes on the path towards the castle. At the top of the rise, she stopped and turned to wave goodbye to Charles but of the monster who had become her friend, teacher, and liberator there was no sign.

"That boy's back," said a voice by her side.

"What boy," replied Eloise as smoothly as if she was still having their conversation that morning in the kitchen.

"Ah," muttered Me, "the boy who came knocking at the castle door, asking for an audience with the princess."

"A boy came knocking at the castle gate asking to see me? You didn't think to tell me this important information?"

"Well," said Me, "I didn't think it was important, he was a nobody."

"A nobody," repeated Eloise. "Why didn't the castle guard report the matter?"

"There wasn't one, just me."

"Then who did the strange boy talk to, to ask for an audience with me?"

"Just me."

"But Me, you're a ghost. No one can see or hear you."

"You can."

"Yes, I know I can, but no one else ever has except Papa and I. Don't you think that's unusual."

"What? That no one can see or hear me?"

"No, silly. That this strange boy can hear you."

"I hadn't thought of that," said Me, "but I still don't think it's important."

"Well you had better take me to him, and we'll find out how important he really is, and how much trouble you are really in."

Eloise had seen the boy who was hanging around the gates outside the castle. She was able to watch him unobserved from high in the castle wall, through an arrow slit which gave a very good view out but with very little chance of being seen. They were designed so that defenders of the castle could shoot arrows out at attackers with no likelihood of being hit in return.

He was quite handsome she thought, in a homely kind of way. Eloise hadn't had the time to bother about boys. She was far too busy riding Rupert, her beautiful horse, or having weapon training with the sword master, or learning magic spells with old Master Zagoop, the castle wizard. Still, she had heard the scullery girls gossiping in the kitchens, and knew most of their talk was about some village boy or other.

The boy was sitting on the edge of an old hay cart watching the castle door and eating a very juicy apple he had been given by a nice old lady whom he had helped with some chores. He watched the soldier in the brightly polished armour, walk smartly out of the castle gate, look around in a searching way, and having alighted his gaze on the boy, march directly towards him in a purposeful manner. The crowd of tradesman, villagers, and ne'er do wells seem to part before him like corn in a field with a charging bull running through it. Taking a last bite from the apple, the boy threw the core away as he jumped down from the wagon and stood tall and proud, unaware of the hidden watcher in the castle above.

The Captain of the guard stood in front of the confident young lad, wondering whatever had got into the mind of young Eloise. Mind she was a confident lass. One day she'll make a worthy successor to her father, the King, he thought.

"Come with me lad," he said to the boy, "I hear you've been making enquiries of the princess."

"Am I in trouble sir?" asked the boy.

"And then some," replied the Captain.

———

The boy had been led by the guard Captain through a labyrinth of corridors until they came to a brightly lit grander passage decorated with sweet scented flowers, and paintings of unicorns and dragons. Finally they came up to a plain oaken door, with a shiny ebony doorknob, that seemed to have been polished by the use of thousands of hands over hundreds of years.

"Wait here," said the Captain, and with a polite nod of his helmeted head took his leave.

With only a few seconds gap, the door opened and there in dirty riding breeches and a leather jerkin stood the princess.

"Actually, it's not even hundreds."

"What," replied the boy, completed wrong footed by this odd greeting.

"The hands that have opened this door. You are correct, it has been here for hundreds of years, but traditionally this room has been the sitting room of the King's eldest child. As I'm an only child that currently is me. By tradition this room is a sanctuary visited only by said eldest child and their maid, or servant, depending on whether they are a girl or a boy. Being an independent young lady I won't have a maid, so the only hand polishing this door knob is mine." This was said in one smooth and flowing delivery.

"You read minds."

"Only recently. I have a new friend and teacher, who only communicates telepathically, and it seems to have rubbed off."

"Isn't that a little rude?"

"Listening to your thoughts."

"Yes."

"I don't pry. Your thoughts broadcasted like you were muttering out loud. If you send a thought my way, I will likely pick it up."

"I'll be careful."

"Always a good tactic. You are clearly an intelligent boy, but you have me at a disadvantage. I am the princess Eloise, who are you."

"The receiver of true loves first kiss."

Eloise burst into peals of laughter and sat down on a very worn embroidered silk sofa with a picture of a golden horse rising up on its hind legs. The boy stood there silently in front of her feeling his cheeks flush red with embarrassment. No one likes being laughed at, especially young men or boys, by the lady or girl of their affections. He watched as Eloise pulled a creased handkerchief from a pocket of her jodhpurs to wipe away her tears of laughter.

"And do you have a name, oh receiver of loves first kiss."

"Oliver," replied the boy, now thoroughly humiliated.

"And where are you from? asked Eloise, who felt bad about Oliver's obvious discomfort, and was feeling rather guilty.

"Gorganland."

"But, that is a land of myth and legend, and said to be a thousand leagues from here. How come you're so far from home."

"It is a long story, my lady."

"Then give me the short version."

"Prince wrongs witch. Witch turns prince into a toad and magics him far away. Princess kisses toad and breaks the spell."

"I remember that toad. That was you? Actually I was going to eat you," she said mischievously, "but didn't like the taste."

"Seemed like a kiss to me," said Oliver, "and it turned me back to a boy."

Eloise couldn't help herself. She broke into fresh fits of giggles, then howls of laughter.

"So now what happens," asked Eloise between guffaws.

"We get married, and live happily ever after."

Eloise was now curled up on the sofa howling with laughter.

"Oh, please stop," she begged, "I can't take any more." She wiped away the tears from her eyes with the now damp handkerchief.

"You're not going to marry him are you," said a voice out of nowhere.

"Oh Me," said Eloise through sobs of laughter, "please go away. No I'm not going to marry him."

"Who is Me?" asked Oliver, "and why aren't you going to marry me?"

Eloise buried her face in the sofa cushions and shook with the continuing flood of her laughter.

"Did you really think I was going to marry you, because I kissed a toad that happened to be a prince?"

"It's tradition," replied Oliver over mouthfuls of cream scone.

"Like having my husband picked for me by my father? That kind of tradition?"

"You know Eloise, Princes waking up sleeping princesses, or rescuing them from fire breathing dragons. Princesses kissing Princes who have been turned into frogs and turning them back into men."

"Well, I'm not a traditional kind of girl," said Eloise, "although I did kill a fire breathing dragon, and rescue the realm when I was ten, and my best friend's a ghost called Me. Still, Oliver, I am only twelve years old. Far too young to get married, and far too sensible."

They were sitting in Eloise's sitting room, side by side on her embroidered sofa, eating buttered scones and lemonade which Eloise had fetched from the castle kitchens. They seemed to be getting on much better now Eloise had recovered from her hysterics.

"And don't you have any real friends?" asked Oliver in a considerate tone.

"Me is a real friend."

"He's a ghost."

"He's a little boy like you. He just happened to die in the castle hundreds of years ago. He's the one who talked to you when you first came to the castle gate."

"The voice in the dark?"

"Yes, he was protecting me. He thought you were a nobody."

"Nonsense," said Oliver firmly, "he didn't want the competition."

"Competition?"

"For your love."

"Oh no," said Eloise, "Me doesn't love me."

"Of course he does," Oliver replied, "but maybe not the way I do."

"Well, you are a Prince," said Eloise sagely. "If Me loves me, it's because he's my friend."

"And what of your new friend, the telepath. What's she like?"

"He is very nice, said Eloise, "although you better be careful if you meet him."

"Why is that," asked the prince."

"Because he's a giant sea serpent who lets me ride on his head on the lake, and teaches me about magic and the world. However he has a wicked side, and eats children. He might eat you."

"Eats children?"

"Yes the first time we met, I was in a boat on the lake, and he smashed it and tried to swallow me whole, but I fought for my life, and survived."

"And now he's your friend"

"Yes, he respects me."

"And your other friend, Me, is happy with this situation?"

"No, said Eloise, "he's just as grumpy about it as I can see you are."

"Well at least we have something in common."

"Aside from loving me."

"Aside from loving you," echoed the prince, taking another bite from his third scone, and picking up his goblet of lemonade. "There is always that."

Me was feeling stretched.

His whole existence had been centred around the castle. In our world, that is ruled by science, and doesn't believe in ghosts, the scientist might say that Me's energy was held and locked into the vicinity of where he died. However Me had never in his conversations with Eloise, shown any awareness either that he had died or that he was not alive in the normal sense of being alive. The fact that no one except Eloise could see him, and that he could pass through walls he just accepted as being a part of his nature. Still, Me the ghost, had never before left the precincts of the castle.

However, never before had Me's best friend, Eloise, princess of the realm, been off making friends with giant magical sea serpents and endangering herself in this way, and Me was off to give Charles a piece of his mind.

"You want me to stop leading Eloise astray?"

"Yes," replied Me from the safety of the shore, "stop filling her mind with all these crazy ideas."

"But Me, you are her friend too, you should be pleased for her."

"Yes, I am her friend, you are not."

"Shouldn't Eloise decide who is and isn't her friend?"

"You are taking advantage of her."

"By teaching her? Enriching her life experience? Teaching her to embrace her potential? How are these not good things?"

"You are a bad creature. You eat dolphins and children."

"I do eat them, it is true. Sharks eat dolphins sometimes, or try to. Lions, and tigers sometimes eat humans. Are they bad? Eloise eats chickens, and sheep. Is she bad?"

"It's not the same."

"Why not," asked Charles.

"Because you are clever and intelligent, and should know better."

"And your friend Eloise, is she not clever and intelligent?"

"Yes, of course she is."

"Then what's the difference."

"It's bad," repeated Me stubbornly, "really bad."

"And, it's bad that I'm Eloise's friend and giving her gifts of understanding and creativity?"

"Yes."

"I thought you were her friend."

"I am," said Me with a note of pride.

"Then act like one."

And with that the great scaly head with the huge penetrating eyes sank down below the surface of the water and was gone.

"I left the castle to meet the monster. He's not your friend."

"Me whatever are you doing?" asked Eloise in a surprised and slightly annoyed voice. "Can't you see I'm busy? I told you to go away."

Me had burst back in to Eloise's special sitting room without knocking or any consideration of what she might of been doing. Now he took stock of the situation, and saw that Eloise and that terrible boy from the gate were sat in comfortable armchairs enjoying a special tea together. Me was so put out and jealous in the moment he almost forgot why he was there. Still he made a fast recovery.

"Aren't you going to introduce me to your friend?" he said, staring rather rudely at the boy.

Eloise after all was a princess, and whatever her feelings about adventures and seeking out unusual friends, she did have impeccable manners. She turned to her guest, making a strong eye contact, and indicating Me with a hand, that still contained a well buttered scone said, "This is my friend Me. I apologise if he has slightly rough and ready ways, he means well and always has my best interests at heart. Me, I believe you have already met Prince Oliver of Gorganland. I accidentally broke the spell that had turned him into a toad, and now he is here to ask for my hand in marriage."

"You kissed a toad?" asked Me incredulously, temporally forgetting all about Charles in his amazement.

"Yes, I did," she replied defiantly.

"Yuk" said Me.

"I didn't know it was a prince," retorted Eloise.

"I am still here," said Oliver.

"Are you inviting Charles to the wedding?" asked Me.

"There isn't going to be a wedding," said Eloise, I'm not going to marry Oliver.

"You seem very well matched," said Me eyeing the remains of an afternoon tea. Being a ghost he wasn't able to share an afternoon tea. "It's traditional, when a princess kisses a frog who turns into a prince.

"That's what I said," said Oliver, slightly put out by the whole conversation. "Who is Charles?"

"He's my friend I mentioned," said Eloise. "And Oliver wasn't a frog he was a toad."

"Doesn't tradition apply to all kissable amphibians? said Me in a smug tone.

"Who is Charles?" repeated Oliver.

"He's my friend."

"He's not your friend," said Me, "He's a giant blood sucking monster who eats children, and I don't like him."

"You don't even know him."

"Yes I do. I talked to him."

"You talked to Charles?"

"Yes."

"Who is Charles?" asked Oliver for the final time, but he was alone. The room vibrated from the slamming of the door. The ghost had vanished and so had Eloise. She was gone.

"So you've met Charles and he's taken you under his wing?"

"Yes, Father."

"And your friend Me, who's a ghost, and a boy who just turned up out of the blue, are both vying for your hand, and are both jealous of, and concerned for your safety with Charles?"

"Yes Father."

And the new boy is a Prince who was changed by a Witch into a toad, whose spell you reversed by kissing him."

"Yes Father, but to be fair I didn't know that he was a prince."

"But you knew he was a toad?"

"Yes."

"And he feels that he has tradition on his side, so you should marry him."

"Yes."

"Which you don't want to, because you're not a traditional girl, and too young to boot?"

"Yes Father."

"And to top it all, Charles is a giant roguish sea serpent who eats children, and at your first encounter tried to eat you?"

"Yes Father."

"Then it seems Eloise, that you are in a bit of a pickle."

ALSO BY RICHARD WEALE

ANN THROPE NOVELS

ASSASSIN

APPRENTICE

POLLY GRANGER NOVEL

THE LIFT

WRITING AS JHEDRON LUCKSPAR

REVENGE OF THE HRYM

EQUATIONS OF BEING (SHORT STORIES)

ASSASSIN

She's a master of the space-time continuum. But with alien mercenaries hot on her high heels, is this assassin's life about to end in a black hole?

Sophisticated grandma Ann Thrope is exceptionally good at murder. The planet's most dangerous professional killer, she's just completed lucrative hits across the cosmos. But when word of her remarkable work spreads through the multiverse, she's saddled with a galactic-sized price on her head...

Continuing to take contracts anywhere and anywhen, Ann continues to dodge an onslaught of extraterrestrial bounty hunters. But when her grandchildren are put in the crosshairs, the stiletto-wielding senior jumps into battle to defend those she loves.

Can this classy hitwoman take down the sinister fiends on her tail before she's permanently retired?

APPRENTICE

He could have been anything when he grew up. Somehow "killer" ended up top of his list...

Young orphan Billy Brambling doesn't believe in being ordinary. Fearing life already passing him by, the eccentric nine-year-old jumps at the chance to learn how to become a deadly assassin. And with his future assured in the lethal hands of infamous hitwoman Ann Thrope, he eagerly begins his career in murder.

Studying under the sophisticated senior, a blind swordmaster, and an eight-inch fairy, Billy focuses on being the most ruthless gun-for-hire across galaxies. But when a dangerous assignment compromises his safety, the youngster must make a life-threatening choice between friend and foe.

Can the boy executioner survive a brutal alien mission, or will he come to an explosive end?

THE LIFT

She went from riding the Tube to traveling the Milky Way. But when an alien admirer sets his sights on her, London might pay the ultimate price.

Polly Granger's life changed the instant she stepped into a London lift. Transported to another realm with two strange men as fellow passengers, she accidentally launches a successful and lucrative career as a dimension-hopping monster slayer. But after five years, a relaxing visit to her luxury Bay Area condo ends abruptly when she sees news footage of a twenty-foot-tall extraterrestrial rampaging through British streets… crying her name.

Shocked when she recognises the otherworldly creature, she's somewhat dismayed to discover its carnage is all in a declaration of love. For her. And now she'd better strap on her weapons before the UK Special Forces decide giving her up is the only option to save them all…

Is this interplanetary badass about to be felled by affection?

ACKNOWLEDGMENTS

Thank You
    Editing by Louise
    Cover art by Fram
    Cover design by Rica

Confession

One of these stories started off as two micro stories in my first published book of short stories, Equations of Being in 2014. I liked them so much, I had thoughts of creating a novel or graphic novel as it's about super heroes. I had completely forgotten about it, and just came across it, on my hard drive, beefed up into a less micro short story. Goddamn pinkos!

Thank you for taking the time to read my book.

Richard 2024